GRABBED BY THE GUARD

SARAH SPADE

FOREWORD

Thank you for checking out *Grabbed by the Guard*!

This is the sixth book in the **Sombra Demons** series and, like the others, can be read as a standalone though it does coincide with the previous book in the series, *Claimed by the Creature*. At the end of Sierra and Dagon's story, it is revealed that Sierra's best friend, Billie—and the heroine of this book—has gone missing after her human (ex)boyfriend Trevor confessed that he was an obsessive fan of Sierra's pop star persona. It is presumed (and then confirmed) that she was taken from their apartment kitchen by Glaine, a recurring character throughout the series who finally gets his own story—and his HEA.

Like the other interconnected standalones in this series, *Grabbed by the Guard* features the fated mates trope, plus a grumpy and possessive (yet utterly devoted) demon, a prickly heroine with her own baggage, a kidnapping followed by a jailbreak that kick off a romance that is super heavy on forced proximity with explicit sex scenes, a little profanity, and a ton of instalove. It's a little angstier than some of the other stories, but if you've wondered about the glowering guard with green eyes who's spent the whole series doing Duke Haures's bidding... this is your chance to learn all about Glaine—and watch a ball-busting heroine in her early thirties show this immortal demon a thing or two!

xoxo,
Sarah

PROLOGUE

GLAINE

If there is one thing I have learned over my existence, it is this: when the opportunity presents itself, take it.

It's how I rose up the ranks to become head of Duke Haures's guard. Same for when I think that I could be toiling away in the stuffy school of mages but for a rare quirk of my birth; born with the mystical second pair of horns but also the tell-tale eyes that mark me as a soldier, I could've been educated or trained. I chose the sword over a tome, and for seven centuries now, I've never once regretted that choice.

No. I've had but a single regret, and as soon as I find the one true mate meant for me alone, even that will be a memory.

It *must* be.

She must be.

But, no. I have been given another, even rarer gift: a second prophecy. And while the seer made it clear that the terms of the first haven't changed—that I am destined to find my mate only for my female to inevitably deny me—I have hope that, with the additional one, I can overcome that.

Even now, I remember it and cling to what I believe it must mean...

> *In chains of gold and magic bound,*
> *You linger close, yet far profound.*
> *To win the heart you hold so dear,*
> *Release the spell that chains you here.*
> *For love's true love is not in grasp,*
> *But in the freedom you grant at last...*

Centuries ago, it was Lucian who saw the first vision and warned me that I would be denied. As a soldier, it was easier to accept the clear and precise warning; as Glaine, it was even easier to dismiss it because I couldn't see how any chosen female would deny me.

The second prophecy was given to me by Damien. Damien, who loves his riddles, and who added a warning of his own: that even when one of his riddles seems straightforward, it isn't, and if Duke Haures hadn't commanded him to read my future in particular, he would've been content to let me continue in my centuries-long search for my one true mate without interfering.

That search ends tonight. At least, I hope so. Following my former fellow soldier's lead, I will risk it all to find the *Grimoire du Sombra*.

It is in the human realm. Sammael stole it himself, telling Duke Haures he would return it before reading the *verus amor* spell to see if he was destined for a human mate. Something told him he must be—though, when I asked if he had met with the doppelseers like I had, he denied *that*—and since I met his Hope myself, he was right.

All I've ever known—courtesy of Lucian's first vision—was that, apart from her being destined to deny me, my female was also fated to be born off-plane. For so long, I believed that meant I would find her in another demon realm. Soleil was my first choice, then maybe Brille Rouge. But in the decades since Duke Haures secreted his human mate to Mavro, with only his guard and a few of his inner circle knowing that Duchess Susanna exists... I've wondered.

Am I also meant to be mated to a mortal?

The scroll with the matefinder spell has long been lost. The only way to discover if a demon's one true mate is a legendary human is to wait and see if we'll be summoned by her, dragged through a portal, and brought to the human world. It is one of Duke Haures's most fiercely enforced laws that Sombra demons cannot go to that world otherwise...

Ah. But I am no regular Sombra demon. I am one of the duke's most trusted guards, and though I do not have the ability to open portals off-plane myself, I am one of the only demons who have been to the human realm and can navigate there.

The *Grimoire du Sombra* is still there. After Sammael found his human mate and decided to hide in the shadows of her home on Earth, he lost possession of the spellbook. He admitted as much to the duke while I was standing behind his throne, but Duke Haures didn't seem to mind.

After all, the book has human magic of its own. Destined to move on to the next mortal female so that she can eventually find the Sombra demon waiting for her in my world, I grumpily settled down to wait and see how many decades it would take until I might have the opportunity I seek.

Mere cycles. That's how long. Mere cycles before the spell summoned another demon I was familiar with: Dagon, Duchess Susanna's personal bodyguard.

Dagon knows where the grimoire is. He must. And though I risk rousing the hunter's protective instincts, approaching him while he is so newly mated with his mortal, I have no other choice. Once they're fully bonded, I will have no excuse to check on them.

Once they're fully bonded, the magic in the spellbook might disappear before I can get my claws on it…

A young mage burrows his own feet claws nervously into the ash. We're on the edge of Mavro, where the capital's blue moon and garden oasis give way to the red sky, fire pits, and ash fields that make up most of our shadowy realm. He's in his solid demon form, purple eyes downcast as though afraid to offend me.

I stand tall and proud, wearing my red skin and onyx horns. I'll have to fade to my shadows once I pass over to the human world; for all that I am risking, I will not risk breaking the duke's first law. For now, I show off my larger size and green soldier's gaze so that Morgath doesn't forget who is asking this favor of him.

"The travel spell is primed," he announces, and I glance down at myself, already noticing the golden runes beginning to hover over my deep red forearm. "Shall I come with you?"

If it was Sammael asking, yes. For centuries, Sammael served as Duke Haures's head mage while I led the guard. We often went to the human world together whenever the duke had cause to send us. Sammael would open the portal, and if I needed him to conjure the enchanted chains that marked a demon as the duke's prisoner, he was there to do so. If not, he waited back in Sombra to trigger the transport spell that would return me home.

But though I leave this eve on the pretense of checking on Dagon and his human mate, Duke Haures did not order me to go. If he did, it would be Loki—Sammael's student, and the former rogue who joined me when I had to take Sammael himself into custody—that was responsible for the chains.

Loki is in Nuit. His human mate is carrying his spawn, and he only leaves her side when the duke commands him to.

The duke didn't command him. In fact, the duke has no idea that I'm taking this trip—though the moment that I do, he will sense it.

In Sombra, Duke Haures can sense *everything*.

I only hope that I can explain myself. That I go in search of my mate, and if I happen to retrieve the grimoire for his grace in the meantime...

It is a flimsy excuse. Duke Haures made an example of Sammael, putting him in chains after he stole the *Grimoire du Sombra* for himself. Demons aren't supposed to meddle in human magic, but all I see is a male who took the chance and who, after his mate went to great lengths to convince Duke Haures to release him from the dungeons, is now happily bonded to her.

There is nothing I won't do to finally have a mate of my own. For all the centuries of service I've offered the duke, he must understand that.

But that doesn't mean that I will drag Morgath into my desperate madness.

"No. Once the portal is open, leave a path for me to return. That's all I need of you."

"Of course, sir."

I clap him on the shoulder. "Thank you."

Morgath looks startled. "Um, well. Yes. You're welcome, sir."

I decide to not comment on his discomfort. Instead, I nod and back away, waiting for the shadows to gather and create the portal for me to jump through.

I know my reputation. I've earned it. I've been loyal to Duke Haures since I came to serve under him, and that loyalty has a price. He took the throne and the crown from our previous ruler two millennia ago, back in the time before I existed, but there have been more than a couple of uprisings in the centuries since I trained as a soldier.

I've squashed them. I've devoted my entire existence to serving the duke, but it's time that I once again look toward the endless centuries in front of me.

I am alone. I am *lonely*. Though many other demons wait just as long as I have to find their one true mate—or even give up the hunt, settling on any demoness who will have his essence—I've only grown more and more determined of late to have mine.

With every human-demon mating that the duke has sent me to warn, I've begun to suspect that, when

Lucian said my mate would be found off-plane, he didn't mean in another demon world. He meant Earth, and that's where I am going now.

Heading through the shadows, I allow the travel spell to guide me toward the essence of Dagon—the last Sombra demon who might know where to find the *Grimoire du Sombra*—until I'm standing on the odd slick flooring that tells me I'm inside one of those over-sized human dwellings.

Two things happen at once: I immediately shift from my solid demon form to my shadows, and I gasp when a sudden realization hits me at the same time as my heart thuds and my cock... for the first time in a long time... my cock starts to harden beneath my shadows.

I came to the human realm in search of Dagon and information on the spellbook.

I came for the book itself—and, instead, my body comes alive as I recognize that the one I've hoped for... the one I've *longed* for... she is *here*.

As my cock continues to stir, my claws curling so that the points disappear past the edge of my shadows, finding meat there to pierce beneath it... as my breath catches and the shadows in front of me are aglow with green as my eyes blaze... as I feel drawn out of my hiding place, an invisible tether tugging me forward even as I dig in my heels... I am stunned that I could ever mistake my attraction to another female as the beginning of a mate bond.

All I have is the echo of my mate's essence and her scent on the still air, and that's enough. I would kill for this mortal. Immortal as I am, I would die if she asked it of me.

I would do anything... anything but release her from this fated tie that I never expected to be as powerful... as all-*consuming*... as it suddenly is.

I've wondered what it was about these human females that made decent and honorable demons seem to lose their minds. Why Malphas was willing to take chains to protect his odd creature, or why Nox *did* take them for many, many cycles. How a colorless, fangless, fragile female was strong enough to turn a rogue demon into a mage again, restoring the purple to his gaze and the sanity to his essence.

And Sammael... educated, learned, powerful Sammael... who spent cycles as a phantom rather than release the sliver of a bond that kept him tethered to a human female he could see but not touch until he found a way around the human's magic...

In a flash, I understand it all. I understand the lengths they have all gone to to claim their mates, and why Duke Haures would go to war with any plane that might even hint at taking offense to a former mortal being Sombra's duchess.

I would do all that and more for a female I have not yet met.

But she is here. I *sense* her. Somewhere in this strange den is my mate. I have no need for the grimoire now, or to confront my fellow demon and demand its whereabouts. Most importantly, I'd rather not confront Dagon at all. He is a hunter. It won't be long until he senses there is another Sombra male near his mate, and whether he is bonded or not, he will be fiercely protective of his female.

I haven't even laid eyes on mine yet and my phantom horns itch to ram against any male that might come between her and I.

Will I challenge Dagon? It is unseemly, especially for a member of Duke Haures's guard. For centuries, I told myself just that when I wondered why I never challenged Apollyon. But as my cock continues to stir against my shadows, pulsing, thickening, growing hard as I sense my mate and ready myself for her... let all the hunters in Sombra stand in my way and I would cast them aside to reach the one my essence calls out for.

It belongs to her. It always has, and though I might have been hasty in trying to give it away over my long existence, I am grateful that I have it to offer to her now.

I have no doubt that she will accept it eventually. That is what human females do. Unlike a demoness, who will recognize a demon as her one true mate and eagerly take both his essence and his cock, the mortals need to be coaxed into understanding their fate. I will have to woo her. To show her how she will want for nothing with Glaine as her mate. To pleasure her and mate her and make her mine.

And I will do that in Sombra while hoping that, this time, she will not deny me...

There is no other option. I belong in my realm. My mate belongs with me. Though I am not a hunter like Dagon, I will join the other shadows in this room and when the opportunity presents itself, I will take it.

If I have to?

I will take *her*.

CHAPTER 1

WORST NIGHT EVER

BILLIE

As I take a wrong step on my way out of the Central Park West Garage and the three-inch heel on my stiletto catches in a crack in the pavement, I can't help but think that tonight can't get any worse.

Even the heel buckling under my weight does little more than have me sighing under my breath. I don't really curse—I leave that to Sierra—but if anything called for a 'damn it', tonight ranks near the top of the list. I'm tired, though. The last time I glanced at my phone before tossing it in my bag and trudging out of the garage, I saw it was already after two in the morning. I should be fast asleep.

Instead, I've just spent a nerve-wracking two hours

driving my rental back to Manhattan from my disaster of a weekend getaway in Connecticut.

I don't like to drive. I can if I have to, but when I'm used to traveling on tour buses and private planes when I'm not living in the capital of public transportation, New York City, it's a miracle I got a license in the first place. Since I spent my seventeenth birthday on stage in Amsterdam, singing "Ooh-bop-bop" with Sierra and Tandy, it's not like I was in any rush like most girls that age. Our next top-ten single was my goal, not cruising around my hometown in a beater my parents would've got from some shady guy for three hundred bucks.

I loved them, but I wanted more than that. I still do. So I got my license after Thr33peat broke up, but before I finished getting my MBA and starting up Bickles Management. So I *can* drive... but it takes a lot of grit and nerve to get me to agree to anything longer than a fifteen-minute ride.

In this case, a mixture of spite and heartbreak got me to the only late-night rental service I could find at the last minute, and three blonde espressos downed one after another was the stimulant I needed to put my heel to the pedal. The nerves would've been enough to keep my eyes open—the memory of Trevor's 'apology' running through my head doing the same thing—but I ordered the coffee anyway because, well, it seemed like a good idea at the time.

Going to Connecticut with that weasel seemed like a good idea at the time.

Leaving Sierra alone with Three in the apartment when I could sense how much she needed me to stay... yeah, I knew that was a bad idea. Especially since I'd put down my fifteen percent for Sierra's last film contract that she called up Jared the second I was out the door, I knew it was a really bad idea.

And, if I'm being honest, I have to admit that going on that weekend trip out of the city with Trevor Daniels when I was working up the nerve to dump him... that was a *terrible* idea.

Our relationship had run its course. A year after we hit it off and started dating, my sixth sense started tingling. It wasn't anything he said or did. At first, I tried to talk myself into accepting that I was overreacting. That just because he was the first long-term relationship I've ever had that didn't get complicated because of my position as *the* Whiskey Rose's manager, it didn't mean anything was suspicious.

Oh, but it *was*. And I'm the idiot who didn't pick up on the—obvious in hindsight—clues that Trevor wasn't just secretly in love with my best friend, he's another one of those obsessed fans that currently have poor Sierra on house arrest in the Dorado.

Crap. How am I going to tell her that, if Trevor's reaction to me immediately breaking things off and warning him away from Sierra is anything to go by, we might have another Patrick Ridgefield on our hands?

Damn it. Damn, damn, damn.

Exhausted and wired, thanks to the espressos, I force myself to stop thinking about that. Ridgefield isn't worth it. Trevor definitely isn't. And if he thinks I'm going to let this go and *not* tell Sierra... I just hope that she decided to ignore my suggestion from the other day when I mentioned she might want to go through her fan mail.

Trevor wrote her love letters. Seriously. Not realizing that a pop star as famous as Whiskey Rose might not handle each piece of fan mail personally, he spent months waiting for her reply. When he didn't get one? That crackpot decided that I'd finally figured out that he was only dating me so that, eventually, Whiskey Rose would notice him.

Because who would ever choose Billie Bickles when the long-reigning princess of pop was right there?

Story of my life.

Snap.

Damn.

Another misstep as I turn the corner, heading for the front of the Dorado. This time, the heel snaps all the way, causing me to stumble and only right myself in time.

It's late, but a lifetime in show biz has my instincts

buzzing. I might not see the paps skulking around right now. Doesn't matter. With as many high-profile residents as the Dorado has, odds are there's usually a camera or two pointing this way. The last thing I need is some Page Six tidbit about one of the former members of Thr33peat hobbling home, visibly drunk, on her way to see the break-out star.

Do they care that I purposely gave up performing myself because I preferred managing? That I'm not going to see Whiskey Rose as an old friend, but because Sierra is my *best* friend and the little sister I never had? That the apartment is much my home as it is hers, and that with both of our love lives a shit show lately, the idea of just settling down with our fluffy-haired void is more and more promising these days?

Ugh.

I have to get inside and quick; hopefully before my photo gets snapped. Sierra doesn't need the drama while she's recovering from her recent scare in California, and I'm dying to change my outfit, throw my wild curls up into a bun, and get my hands on the mail bags.

One upside to the espresso shots? I'm not going to sleep anytime soon, and since I spent the drive back into the city determined to get my hands on Trevor's letters before Sierra had to deal with it, that's exactly what I'm going to do.

But, first, these stupid heels—

The skirt on my tight red dress is riding up as I

crouch down, reaching for the snapped stiletto while trying not to whack myself with my bag. It's the Prada Sierra bought me last Christmas, and while part of me wanted to brain Trevor over the head with it—and it's big and heavy enough to do it—I would never harm one of my precious babies by using it on a worthless creep who doesn't deserve it.

Considering how much Sierra splurged to buy it for me, it also doesn't deserve to be set down on the middle of a Manhattan sidewalk—on the UWS or not. I totter on the good heel, struggling to balance without dropping my bag, and get the shoe off. Tucking the busted heel under my arm, I do the same to the other since walking with one three-inch heel on, one off, would only draw out the photogs looking for a tipsy B-list celeb.

One problem. Naive Billie didn't bother with stockings earlier tonight when Trevor mentioned I should dress up nice for dinner. Assuming dinner would lead to sex since the weekend had been going okay up until that point, I didn't want to waste time removing them later.

Of course, instead of sex, Trevor decided to accuse me of wanting to keep Whiskey all to myself once we were back at the rented house—and it took longer than it should've for me to realize he meant Sierra and not a bottle of booze. When I finally decided I'd had enough and I was leaving, I grabbed my suitcase, my purse, and my heels.

I regret that now as my bare feet settle on the chilly —and questionable—sidewalk. It's November, so it's not snow-covered or anything, but that only makes it worse that my feet are damp.

Ah, well. You can scrub your feet. A Prada tote? I wouldn't dare.

I move faster without the heels. Before I know it, I'm nodding at the night-time doorman on duty in front of our building. Karl murmurs a greeting, careful not to use my name in case my picture was snapped and some young pap after my time might not recognize my face.

Then I remember that my trademark wild curls are all they need to know who I am...

I slip inside, heading right for the elevator. The apartment I share with Sierra—that *is* Sierra's, but she'll go off in a snit if I ever admit that that's how I see it—is a classic six, one floor below the penthouse. During the day, a concierge will join me on the ride up so that I can access my floor. After hours, so long as the doorman lets you in, you're on your own.

As soon as I'm home, I exhale. Oh, the coffee still has me jittery, and I really, really don't want to have this conversation with Sierra, but I'm home. Keeping my Prada bag on my shoulder, I toss my shoes along the hall.

With Gladys and Maurice on vacation while Sierra's tour is on pause, I don't feel so guilty leaving them there for either our housekeeper or our house sitter to find.

I'll look into getting my stiletto repaired tomorrow. And, seeing how the entire apartment is quiet and dark, I'm thinking about postponing my conversation with Sierra until then, too.

The idea of keeping the truth from her never occurs to me. She likes to tease that I'm honest to a fault, the real goody-goody from our time in Thr33peat, and maybe that's true. I'm also loyal to my best friend —hell, my *only* friend—and, with her being two years younger than me, I'm very, very protective.

I also recognize that Sierra is thirty-one, and that she's been independent for a long time. My parents were a lost cause by the time Thr33peat was my only shot at survival, with my dad doing time for possession and my mom the one who kept possessing after he was gone, but Sierra ended up emancipated from her momager before she was sixteen. To hide this from her wouldn't only be dangerous, considering her history with obsessed fans turned dangerous stalkers, but it would also be patronizing.

Doesn't mean that it can't wait until morning. I still want to find the letters and see how bad they are. Now that my 'manager' brain is kicking in, I'm sure they're bad—just as much as I'm sure that Sierra didn't stumble across them yet in the, like, nine bags of fan mail I arranged for her to have as a distraction from her recent vocal rest.

She's been so down lately, I thought she might need a reminder why the world loves Whiskey Rose as much as I adore my best friend. The team I put in charge of the fan mail is careful to pull out anything that might be a threat to her, but since *I* didn't know about Trevor's letters until he mentioned them, they have to still be in there. And while Sierra was a lot quieter this weekend than usual, texting me sporadically as if she was definitely distracted, I'm beginning to understand why... and I don't think her going through her fan mail is as much of a concern anymore.

Peering down the hall, through the open study, I see that her bedroom door is closed. I'm in a foul mood, and I'm not sure if my reaction is to roll my eyes because my suspicion is right—or sigh again because it has to be.

Sierra is an open book, but if I've learned anything over the years as her roommate, it's that a closed door means she needs privacy. If it's open, it's an invitation for people to approach her. If it's closed, stay out.

The staff are all on break while Sierra's recovering. Even Roy—our longtime head of security—is staying off-site. I texted Sierra hours ago that I would be coming home a day earlier from my getaway and that we'd talk... and her door is closed.

The only reason it would be is if she has a guy

sleeping over. And normally I wouldn't care—my need to get laid is what got me so involved with Trevor Daniels in the first place—but Sierra... she's too famous for one-night-stands.

I shudder out a breath of pure annoyance.

Jared Turner is in there, isn't he?

Settling for rolling my eyes, I trudge toward the kitchen. Right now, with the night not even close to being over, I need an aspirin. Too much caffeine plus my anxiety going through the roof and I've got one hell of a headache brewing. I have some aspirin in my bag, but I'll need some water to swallow it down.

Then I can swap my dress for some sweats and hunker down in the study for a little one-on-one time with Sierra's fan mail.

Anything to stop Trevor's pleading voice from echoing in my ears...

You had to know, Billie. You're a nice girl, and we had fun, but you had to know that it's always been Whiskey...

I plop my tote on the kitchen table with more force than I mean to, then feel guilty a second later. I've never once been jealous of Sierra. Even after Trevor revealed just how disgusting and twisted he is, I would never blame her for being America's sweetheart. As always, my main concern is *for* her—

"That's it," I grumble under my breath, voice sounding shaky and echoing in the quiet. "I'm done. No more men for me. Sierra can keep Three, I'll adopt

Four and Five if I have to, and I'll be a childless cat lady."

Sounds like a perfect plan to me—

The little hairs on the back of my neck stand up. I don't know why. Between reliving Patrick Ridgefield's attempt on Sierra's life and imagining Trevor holding the gun instead on my nerve-wracking drive home, I'm already on edge. Toss in the caffeine and what's quickly becoming one of the worst nights ever, and my imagination is in hyperdrive.

Is someone behind me?

I... it seems like someone might be behind me.

It's not Three. I haven't seen any sign of our cat since I entered the apartment. Usually he'll beg for treats from anyone, no matter the hour, so the fact that he hasn't tells me that he got trapped in Sierra's room when she closed the door. Luckily, there's an extra litter box in the bathroom for occasions just like that, but poor Three if he got a front-row seat to a naked Jared Turner.

And that's not really fair of me. There's a reason why Jared—with his dimpled chin and pretty boy style —is as famous as Sierra. He's got the looks, the talent, and the charm... plus the inability to keep his dick in his pants so, never mind, maybe it is very fair of me.

But all that to say... no. The darkening shadows that have caught my attention out of the corner of my eye are way too big to belong to a nine-pound house cat, no matter how fluffy Three is. Looks even bigger than it should if it belonged to another person, even a pretty tall man, and that just makes me chide myself as I start to turn away from the table, ready to reach for a glass to get some water.

I pause, squinting into the shadows.

Green lights? What the... why are there two green pinpoints floating in the shadows about a foot-and-a-half over my head?

The shadows move, my mind goes blank, and when I have the ability to think again, it's this:

Be careful what you wish for, Billie.

Could tonight get any worse? I didn't think so, but tell that to the massive *monster* that just stepped out of the shadows.

CHAPTER 2
BLUFFING

BILLIE

Should I have screamed? I feel like I should've screamed. Most people probably would have. If I wasn't already at the end of my rope after a long, crappy day, sure, I could pretend to be an actress like Sierra and do 'damsel-in-distress'... and who am I kidding? I've always been more like Megara in *Hercules* when I find myself in any kind of trouble.

I'm a damsel.

I'm in distress.

I can handle this.

By 'handle this', I mean backing up a few steps so that I can take the monster in properly. At least then I can get a better idea if I should be shitting my metaphorical pants, grabbing a knife from the butcher block to protect me, Sierra, and Three (sorry, Jared), or admitting that I've finally lost it.

Another glimpse at the towering figure and I think: why not all of them?

Up until a year or so ago, I would've said that there isn't anything that scares me. I've worked too hard and accomplished too much to let something like fear stop me. Then I watched as Patrick Ridgefield aimed a gun at Sierra and I realized that losing her... that being completely on my own... is the one thing that gets my palms sweaty and my heart rate kicking up.

Now? I can add coming face-to-face with *this* to my list.

I can't really make out too many details in the gloom of the kitchen. The tiny light over the range that never goes out is all I have, but it's enough to give me an outline. A shape. An idea of what the hell I'm looking at.

Honestly? 'Hell' might be right.

The monster is at least seven feet tall if I use the positioning of his glowing green eyes as a gauge for his height. His skin is a dark color, maybe brown, maybe red, and the sculpted muscles on his bare chest—coupled with his imposing size—make it obvious that, whatever he is, he is a guy. A male monster.

His lower half disappears into the shadows, hiding anything below mid-torso. Does he have a forked tail? Cloven hooves? Between the reddish—I'm pretty sure the shade of his skin is closer to rust than anything else —skin and black horns arcing over his head, my brain provides the word 'devil'.

Or maybe 'demon'?

He's a big-ass demon. Twice as wide as me, more than a foot-and-a-half taller, he looms on the opposite side of the kitchen table, watching me with those unblinking green eyes.

He opens his mouth. To say something? To roar? Could be, but I get a glimpse of thick fangs, a black mouth, and a claw-tipped hand heading my way as he reaches out—and I don't scream.

But I do put on my 'manager' voice.

Forget the fact that I'm in my bare feet and a slinky red dress that barely covers me from butt to boob. My hands perch on my hips as I give my head a royal shake, my curls bouncing into my face as I tilt my nose up at him.

"I don't know who you think you are or what you're doing in Whiskey Rose's private apartment, but this is unacceptable." Freeing one hand, treating this giant monster as though he's as much a nuisance as Three running under my step, looking to scrounge up an extra treat, I shoo at him. "Go. Turn around and wherever you came from, you better go back there."

Now, did I honestly think that was going to work? No. I'm just buying time, trying to figure out how to get out of this mess. There's no doubt in my mind that if demons are real and someone somehow found a way to summon one here, it's because they're looking for Sierra.

Over my dead body.

Would reaching for my phone be worth it? I have hundreds of contacts in there—everything from entertainment lawyers to PR specialists and the top security firms that money can buy—but what are the odds that I can pull up someone with the experience I need for… what? An exorcism?

If only I had Father Anthony's number stored in my phone…

I'm going to need something. If my insane hunch is right and I'm dealing with a demon, there's got to be some kind of guide to sending him back where he came from. Shooing him away like he's a stray cat obviously didn't work. He's still watching me without saying a word—and who's to say that he has any idea what *I* am or what I'm saying?

Screw it. Like I said, there isn't anything I can't accomplish with a little grit and my phone. I don't want to get too close to this guy, but with my phone still in my tote, it's worth inching closer to the bag and grabbing it.

Believe me, I'll feel a lot more in control if I have my phone—

"Uxor mi," rumbles the demon in a notably deep voice. "Aver."

I freeze. What did he say?

He repeats the first three syllables, then follows it with quite a few more. I give up paying close attention after it becomes clear that I have no clue what he's saying. That's odd, too. One of the things that had me signing up for Thr33peat in the first place was the chance to see the world, to learn new cultures and customs... and languages.

I'm not saying I'm fluent in many. Proficient in a couple, yes, and it's enough to know that nothing he is saying to me is registering at all.

He is speaking, though. There's an almost dominant tone to his words. Like he's trying to explain something or tell me something and that he expects me to understand.

To understand and, from the imperious expression on his face, *obey*.

Fat chance, demon boy.

Okay. I'm sorry. I'm not in the mood for this. I broke the heel on my shoe, discovered the guy I was sleeping with would pretend I was my best friend when he was banging me, and now there is a demon in my kitchen who thinks he can clack his claws together, gesture in front of him, and I'll listen? Because that's what he's doing now. As if realizing he couldn't understand my English gibberish so I'm probably not fluent in 'demon', he's using universal gestures: snapping his fingers and pointing.

Sure. With fangs like those, does he want me to grab some salt from the counter to season myself up before he takes a bite?

Is that what demons do? Do they eat girls? If he's hankering for a virgin, he's out of luck here. With Sierra probably dozing off with Jared in the other room, and me wishing I'd never let Trevor touch me, there aren't any bashful, blushing virgins in this apartment.

Okay. I've lost it. That's a fair assessment of everything that's happened to me tonight. I'm thirty-three. I've been in show biz for twenty years, give or take. I've never done drugs. Barely drink alcohol. I was always discreet with my lovers. Never had a meltdown. Never needed a psychiatrist of my own.

I think I'm due a bit of a breakdown.

My knees buckle, something I'll privately curse about later. I'd already planned to make another move for my bag, desperate for my phone. Part of me is thinking about looking up symptoms of a stress-induced breakdown. Another part of me is wondering what I'd need to type into the search bar to get instructions on banishing a demon without being put on some kind of a watch list. A tinier part is curious enough to engage my translator app and see if 'demon that suddenly appeared in my apartment for no logical reason' is a setting.

The internet is vast. I'm amazed on a daily basis by

the knowledge at my fingertips in such a tiny device. Who knows? If this is really happening, I doubt I'm the first person in history it's happened *to*.

And if it's *not* happening...

My knees buckle, and I start to pitch forward. That's when I discover just how fast a demon is. For a creature his size, he should lumber. He doesn't. He flies toward me, faster than I can even see him move, and suddenly he's there. One catcher mitt-sized hand grabs me by the upper arm, hoisting me back to my feet before I fall flat on my face.

And without letting go, he says that same word from before. "Uxor."

He looks down at me expectantly. As though I should thank him for man-handling... *demon*-handling me, or if his touch on my arm is supposed to *do* something. All it does is make me realize that demons run at a way hotter temperature than humans do, and while he's not burning my arm, he needs to let go.

Now.

"Let go of me," I tell him, jerking my arm out of his hold.

He doesn't.

This close, I can make out a couple of rows of ridges over his nose and on his brow. They seem to crease as his face sets, cheeks hollowing as the big demon tightens his jaw *and* his grip.

His green eyes glow even brighter, and on his arms, unfamiliar golden runes appear over his *black* skin.

What the—

His hand is still on my arm. I feel it, though I don't see it as, suddenly, the red-skinned demon disappears into an oversized mass of black shadows. It's like a silhouette of where he was with only the green eyes and golden runes to prove he's still there somewhere.

And that's when he tugs on my arm.

I struggle, but I don't scream. This time I don't because the last thing I want to do is wake up Sierra and Three in time for them to see me being *abducted* by this demon. I don't want the monster to make them another target, either, though if Jared got caught in the crosshairs... well, that would be a shame, wouldn't it?

No. I'm not just Sierra's manager. I'm her best friend, and her older sister figure. Though I'm sure she has to be the target, I'll do what I've always done: I'll take care of this insanity, one way or another.

Hey... it can't be any worse than the time Tandy and Sierra almost got the three of us banned from Amsterdam after that Thr33peat show, can it?

So I don't scream, though I do struggle, and as he yanks me forward, pulling me with him into a patch of impossibly black darkness in the corner of my kitchen, my biggest regret is that I never got the chance to grab my phone before I'm swallowed up by it.

BENEATH THE FACADE OF BILLIE THE MANAGER, BILLIE herself can be very reactive. An example? The moment the world stops spinning, my eyes don't seem blacked-out anymore, and my feet sink into something that's both pillowy and kind of sandy, I start slapping at the big, meaty forearm that is holding me pressed against a hard chest.

Clearly surprised by my display of violence, the demon releases me.

I spin on my heel and smack his arm again.

"How dare you? You don't just grab a person and—"

It takes a second for my brain to catch up to my eyes, and for my mouth to register what I'm seeing. Just for fun, my nose decides to come online and, as I suck in a shocked breath, I gasp and choke as the stink of a thousand rotten eggs singe my poor nostrils.

"Oh my God! What is that?"

Faced with such an awful odor, all media training flies out the window. I've spent years learning to think first, speak second, but when all I can think is how much it stinks all of a sudden, I can't help it. My hand flies to my face, shielding my nose and my mouth, but the damage is done.

It's hot, too. Really hot. Like I've walked out of the air-conditioned lobby of the Dorado and into a muggy

August afternoon even though it's still November. This is a dry heat that surrounds me, and to add insult to injury, I can just feel my curls wilting.

I take a step. The ground is uneven. I bobble, jerking away from the demon before he can grab my arm again. Once I have my footing, I glare down at the dirt.

Only it's not dirt. It's *ash*.

Why does it look like I'm standing in the middle of the world's biggest ashtray?

My head jerks up. And then up some more.

Shoving my curls out of my face, I goggle up at the sky.

Even if I wanted to be delusional and pretend that it was possible for the demon to pull me out of my kitchen and to the outside, I'm slapped in the face with a little bit of reality when I see that there are two moons high over my head: one that is full and cast with a reddish tinge, and another that is about halfway full and is *gold*.

I've heard of there being such a thing as a blue moon, but a red one? A gold one?

Two moons?

Okay. *Okay.* So this demon... he definitely stole me. He said something in his demon language, he grabbed my arm, and he brought me here for reasons I can't tell. And while normally my inquisitive side would be all for the adventure, all for learning about this strange not-Earth world he's brought me to, this demon got me on the wrong day.

I glare over at him, wordlessly warning him to keep his distance, then tromp around in the ash. That patch of darkness dragged me here. It must've swallowed the demon up first and that's why I thought he went black; he's back to being the red-skinned, giant demon with the glowing green eyes, though the golden runes are gone now. But if that patch was some kind of pathway between this weirdo demon world and my apartment, if I find it again, I should be able to go home.

Makes sense to me. Too bad that it's not that easy. I mean, the entire terrain around me seems flat and mixed with shades of red, black, and grey, with shadows every-freaking-where... but nothing like that patch that was in my kitchen.

Is it gone? How do I get it back?

Can I—

There's that prickle on the back of my neck again.

I whip my head around.

He didn't move. I'm almost positive he didn't move an inch. That only annoys me more because it's like I could just *sense* him right there behind me.

Our eyes lock, and this time he does lean in my direction.

"No," I snap. I wag my pointer finger at him. Even if he doesn't understand 'no', he should understand that. "No!"

The demon growls softly, a rumble that begins deep in his chest.

I quirk my eyebrow at him. "Is that supposed to intimidate me?" I ask. So he can't understand me... I feel better for filling the stifling quiet with my voice. "I was in a girl group in my teens with Tandy Lewis. Please. If she didn't scare me into a convent, you don't have a prayer."

And, okay. I'm kind of bluffing a little. My mind's running a mile a minute, trying to figure out where I am, why I'm here, and how I'm going to fix this situation *when I don't have my goddamn phone.* But bluffing usually works, and until I can guarantee that a little Billie snack isn't off the table, I'll use whatever advantage I have to keep him over there.

Especially since, now that there are *two* moons giving me a little more illumination than my shadowed kitchen, I'm beginning to second-guess my initial impression.

If this big monster looks hungry, I don't think it's because he wants to eat me. At least, not for dinner.

It's in the way his eyes are watching me. The way his nostrils flare. The way he tilts his head just so, his long black hair falling down his back while his horns are angled in a way that might be attractive to a female of his kind. His bare chest is heaving slightly, his big hands balled into fists as though that's the one way he can remember to keep them to himself, and his lips...

they're thinned, a flash of fang revealed as he turns his growl into a soft sigh.

So he's exasperated with me. I spend all of my time with Sierra; I'm used to that. But there's more to it.

He's a demon. Obviously. He's still a guy—and whether he thinks I look as weird to him as he looks monstrous and demonic to me, I don't think he cares one bit.

And, suddenly, I'm not so sure I can handle this... handle *him*... after all.

CHAPTER 3
ESSENCE

GLAINE

I should have known better than to assume my mate would recognize me as her male and fall into my arms.

I'd made that same mistake once before, and am grateful that Lilith's reluctance to agree that she felt some kind of tie between us kept me from sharing my essence with her right away. She agreed to join me in Sombra, leaving Soleil behind, to give me the chance to woo her—and denied me mere cycles later when she was introduced to my clan leader and realized that *Apollyon* was her one true mate.

That tie I sensed? She believes it was because I was fated to find her in Soleil and bring her to my world so that she could meet Apollyon. Centuries later on from my failure, I still don't know if it was the beginning of a mate bond I felt—or just the first time I was attracted to a female.

Such is life in the barracks. I left Nuit as little more than a spawn, relocating to Mavro so that I could begin my training. At the time, Duke Haures had no mate. His entire staff was made up of demon males, and most demonesses were bonded mates in the village when I would return to Nuit to visit.

Not that I paid the few demonesses who weren't any mind. The doppelseers assured me that my mate would be found off-plane, and when I didn't find a demoness who called to me during any of the campaigns Duke Haures sent me on, I received a year's reprieve to search on my own.

Of course, then she denied me, choosing Apollyon as her bonded mate, and I returned to command well before I was expected to. I've never asked for another leave since, though now that I have my human female with me... I will have to at the earliest opportunity.

But, first, I need to find a way to communicate with my mortal.

I have my essence still—otherwise I would not be able to bond her to me, and now that I'm certain she's mine, I *must*—but, to my wonder and dismay, so does she. I'd thought that, when I took her arm and held her close, she'd instantly know I am her male and pass it along to me.

That… is not what happened.

I had carried her through the portal with me, bringing her to Sombra, and once we landed on the outskirts of Mavro, I waited for her to give me her essence. She struck me instead. It didn't hurt, and I almost thought she was being a playful little human—and then I saw the unmistakable fury on her adorable face.

I have not met many humans, but I think it is fair to say that she is the most attractive of her kind. Everything about her is attractive to me. Her dim yet pretty blue eyes, the same shade as Duke Haures's. Yellow ringlets that bounce every time she moves—and a pair of bountiful breasts that, yes, also seem to bounce as she paces away from me. She's wearing a slip of a covering, showing off a human form that is so different than that of a demoness. If a male didn't know his own strength, she could be broken in half, she's that fragile, and her missing horns are surprisingly *erotic* to me.

The first time I laid eyes on the mortals, when Duke Haures found his duchess, I admittedly found them strange to look at. They're soft-looking. Squishy. Weak. Where were the points on their ears? The ridges on their brow? Horns to protect their skulls?

True, instead of horns to battle with, they have

breasts to snare their males. They are small, but with a Sombra demon as a mate, they are fiercely protected. Their eyes don't shine with any light to give insight into their nature, but with Susanna first, then when I had the... pleasure to meet Malphas's mate, I learned that humans are different, yet vibrant and alive even so.

I wonder what I will learn about my mate...

But that is my biggest problem. With her essence, I would know it all, but she hasn't shared it. And when I showed my frustration by letting out a soft growl, she spoke at me in her human language.

I know little of it. The duke and duchess sometimes murmur to each other in her tongue, but what they speak of is not my concern. I never thought there would be a reason for me to learn any of those words, especially when a mortal mate would instinctively learn Sombran as soon as she took her male's essence.

I can tell from her tone that she is not happy with me. That is the last thing I want. My mate should be pleased to see me, not glaring daggers at me with her dark gaze as she spins on her heel, pointing at my chest.

"Dnt knoweer iam," she says, and there's a ferocity to the nonsense words that makes my aching cock twitch. I weave another layer of shadow over my lower half to conceal it. Angry as she is, I don't want my mortal to think I only want to lie with her, instead of making her my forever partner for the rest of my immortal existence. "U kant ex plane cuz idnt knowat ursayin."

Is she upset that the essence exchange didn't work? She was in the same quarters where I sensed Dagon's essence. The way she reacted upon seeing me—with more curiosity than fright—makes me wonder if she knew about Sombra demons already. She can't be Dagon's mate because she is mine, but what of her kin? The duchess of Sombra's kin was meant for a Sombra hunter years after Duke Haures bonded Susanna to him. Is that what happened? My mate is kin to Dagon's mate and that's why she was there when I went in search of my fellow demon? Does she know of Dagon's human mate—because he has to have one if the *verus amor* spell summoned him to Earth—and wonders why I am different?

Without her essence, I don't know. Even if I offered her mine, that would only allow my mortal into my thoughts. I would have no advantage. I *need* an advantage. There is no way I can risk my mate denying me again. If I lose my essence, I will never have one.

So I must take hers.

Perhaps... perhaps it is because I took her arm. It was not a touch freely given. If she approaches me, taking my hand... would that trigger the exchange?

It's worth a chance.

While I stare at my mortal beauty, making sense of my next actions, she glances over her shoulder. The first part of her mumblings are too muffled for me to hear, before she adds, "Im stuk."

I make a small sound in the back of my throat. It is a soothing sound, meant to calm her without reminding her that the only words I know are in Sombran.

She squints at me. "Thisssis urfult."

Whatever you say, my mortal.

I will be contrite. Using gestures instead of words, I will implore her to at least give me her essence so that I can explain to her who I am, who she is to me, and why I brought her to Sombra with me.

Once she knows that I am her one true mate, she will understand. I'm sure of it.

Bowing my head, regretting for one of the only times in my life that I do not have my second pair of horns in order to impress her with them, I hold out my arm. I wiggle my fingers, letting her see how strong and thick my claws are since I don't think showing off my cock will work just yet. Maybe when we are alone in the privacy of my quarters.

For now, I offer her my skin.

Her gaze is locked on my fingers. Not my fierce claws, but my hand on its own.

"Wat? Troos? Isdat watchu meen?"

"I want you to give me your essence, my mate. Won't you?"

She doesn't understand my words, but my cajoling tone does the trick. Her expression is distrustful, but as though she can sense that she is safe with me, that I will not harm her, she moves until she's right in front of me.

Lifting her arm, she keeps her own hand tucked near her breasts. I'd once thought the pale pink coloring of humans like Susanna meant they were sick. I no longer do. She is healthy for a being that can perish, and I look forward to the moment when our bond will make her immortal.

"Please," I rumble.

Perhaps she understands some Sombran after all. That, or my pleading sways her. Either way, she darts out her hand, pressing her palm against mine before making a strange shaking motion with her arm.

I want to tell her that she need not do that to pass me her essence. Just her willing touch, flesh against flesh, completes the essence exchange.

That's not all that happens. Before, I was too focused on bringing her into the shadows that would lead us to Sombra to notice how different her temperature is from mine. Once we're bonded and she becomes immortal, she will match my heat. For now, her skin is chilled, ripping a gentle moan from me and sending shivers down my spine.

Is it the moan? Or the way my fangs flash as I arch under her touch? As her essence floods through me, filling me up from foot to horn, my first impression is that I've done something wrong. She's frightened... no, she's *angered*.

"What the *fuck*?"

My mortal rips her hand out of my hold. Courtesy of her essence, I easily translate her English expletive into Sombran. That one word—*fuck*—means the act of mating in her language, and I grin.

See? That's all it took. My mate gave me her essence and already understands that she is, in fact, my mate.

"I appreciate your enthusiasm, female, but I think we should wait until we're in Nuit before we learn each other's bodies." However, if she wants to make sure that I can pleasure her... I gesture at my shadow coverings. "But if you'd like me to assure you that I have a cock, I can show it to you now."

Her mouth falls open. "Are you... did you... no! Keep your pants on, you demon perv!"

Perv? I don't know that word. "I am not a perv. I am a guard—and your mate."

She scoffs. "Whatever you say. It doesn't matter. I don't know what happened or why you pretended not to know English until right this second, but I don't care. I'm probably hallucinating this anyway."

Hallucinating? Oh. Seeing things that do not exist.

"This is all real," I tell her. Dropping low, I scoop up some of the ash from the local ash field. Rising again, I let it fall from my palm. "We are in Sombra."

Crossing her arms over her delectable chest, she snaps, "I don't know what Sombra is, either, but it's not New York and that's all I care about. So if you'll just get that patch of darkness back so I can go home... that would be great. Yeah?"

The patch of darkness she's referring to is the travel spell that brings a demon from Sombra to another plane.

"Why would I do that? I only just retrieved you, mortal."

"And? You can bring me back."

I set my jaw. "I will not. I went to the human realm for my mate. I found her. Now you'll stay with me."

She blinks. I've surprised her, and I can sense her changing tactics at my blunt refusal to let her go. I haven't been able to delve into her essence enough to learn much about my mate, but it's clear that she is stubborn like her male—and she proves it when she says, "Well, sorry, but you got the wrong girl. I'm not Sierra."

"Not-Sierra? That is your name?"

I know her human tongue... why don't I know her name?

"What? No. I'm Billie... but that's my point. I'm Billie. I'm not Sierra."

What is a Sierra?

Her essence... the exchange is complete, but she has somehow managed to conceal much of herself.

That interests me as much as it frustrates me. As she is my mate, I want to know everything about her, but as a soldier who knows better than to share his essence freely, I am pleased that she is smart enough to hold some of herself back. She's become someone that I can study, a female to learn, and I look forward to that almost as much as I do the moment when she will give up denying that she is mine and welcome me into her heart—and her cunt.

I close my eyes, attempting to focus. Learning about your mate through their essence is supposed to be as instinctive as breathing for a Sombra demon. And yet... though I have hers, it seems as though it's been protected behind a wall.

Sierra... I see a human female with honey-colored eyes and hair like a length of twine tossed over her delicate shoulder. My mate is fond of her, and this other mortal is one of my mate's motivations to return to Man-hat-tan. New York. Her clan.

She needs to speak with her... the word I think means 'friend', but it seems more like kin. As though they are family. My Billie has to warn her about...

Trevor.

What is a *Trevor* now?

I delve deeper, claws curling to pierce my palms,

my hands fisting as another image flashes through my mind. It's of another mortal, male this time, and he's... he's...

I snarl, banishing the memory of another male pleasuring my mate. I shove the rest of her essence to the corner of my mind, no longer wanting to see. She is *my* female. *My* mate. I made no mistake. I knew from the moment I caught her scent and felt the echoes of her essence brush up against me that *Billie* was born to belong to me. Whether she's had other males before, it matters not. I am her male now.

I open my eyes, ready to face her and, in her tongue, explain that I am her one true mate—and I roar.

She is *gone*.

She won't get far. I have her essence, and even if I didn't, we are mates. Our bond is not finalized, but it exists. I will follow her anywhere, and not only because—as a Sombra demon—my nature compels it.

I have no doubt that she believes she will find a portal to take her back to the human world if she goes off in search of one. She's wrong. Only a mage can rip a hole between worlds to return her. And while there are plenty of mages inside of Mavro, she would have to know how to find her way to the capital city first—and survive the shadow beasts and rogue demons that lurk in the darkest of Sombra's shadows.

In the distance, I see the silhouette of my wee

mortal, illuminated by the orange glow from the fire pits. That's another danger. She could fall into the fire, her mortal body burning away, just more ash for the fields.

No.

I sprint after her, and between my stride and my speed, I catch up to her almost immediately. Plus, I notice as I reach her, she has stopped running, making my pursuit of her all the easier.

I thought it was the fire pit that stopped her. When Billie yelps and, to my surprise, darts behind me, I see what *did* pause her in her flight.

Vorn. A guard two centuries my younger who I've known nearly as long.

His green eyes brighten when he sees me. "Glaine. You've found the trespasser."

"Oh, no," my mortal mutters behind me. "Can this get any worse?" A hollow laugh, followed by, "Really? I've already tempted fate once and got knocked on my ass for it. Do I really want to see how much worse things can get?"

Her words are not meant for me. Still, I move my hand behind me, gesturing to her that I am here, and I will protect her from my fellow guard.

"Trespasser? What trespasser?"

Vorn tilts his head, the flame from the fire pit reflecting off of his polished horn. "The creature tucked behind you, Glaine. She is small, but you must have seen her." He lowers his voice. "She resembles the duchess."

Yes. Because she is human. "That doesn't make her a trespasser."

I step forward so that the young demon knows better than to move toward my Billie. So that he understands I'm not here to help him apprehend her, but to keep her safe from him.

She doesn't have my essence. She only knows that I'm speaking in Sombran—but then she gulps audibly, and when she moves closer, laying her hands on the small of my back, I'm resolved. Let Vorn attempt to reach for my mortal. I will shift to my shadows, retrieve my silver blade from the pocket where I keep it tucked out of sight, and wield it against him.

Does he know that I am one of the rare soldiers who have a sword given to them by Duke Haures himself? One that, with the perfect strike, will end even an immortal's existence without being abandoned to the shadows first?

It was a gift and a duty from his grace when I accepted the post as the head of his personal guard. If a demon goes fully demonic, the silver blade will end him before he becomes a threat to the rest of Sombra. If he rises up against the duke, I have the authority to cut him down.

If Vorn attacks my Billie—

He holds up his hands, a warding-off gesture. "I beg

your forgiveness, sir. Duke Haures warned that there was a threat to the duchess's safety on the grounds outside of the palace."

I long to bare my fangs at him, but I restrain my anger. Instead, I gesture behind me. "She is a mortal. What kind of threat is she to demonkind?"

Vorn gulps, but I'll give the lad credit. He doesn't falter. "It doesn't matter. The duke's orders were clear."

"What's going on?" Her breath is cool on my skin as she whispers in English to me. I understand that she's confused and possibly startled by Vorn's sudden appearance, but my fellow soldier can only speak in Sombran. Unless I tell her what it is that he's said—or who he is—then she cannot tell for herself, and she proves that when she edges closer, asking, "Who is he? What does he want?"

I don't want to hurt Billie, but I act as if I don't understand her human words. Only for a moment, though, because I'd like to know more about what Duke Haures has told Vorn about the 'threatening' female.

"And if she is a mate?" I ask.

What I mean is: do you know that this mortal is mine? If I show to the other soldier that I understand her human tongue when I never have before this eve, it wouldn't take the smartest of males to guess that I am hers.

Vorn is more clever than I thought. He glances to

my side, peeking at Billie, then meets my gaze. His tone turns apologetic yet firm. "If she is, there is no bond. Duke Haures would have sensed it and known there was no threat. If there was no threat, I would not have been ordered to bring the female straight to him."

Godsdamn it. Vorn is right. Just like the duke can tell when the portal between realms has been opened, his specific magic makes it so that he can tell when a bond exists. Of course. He is a bondmaster.

He is also the ruler of Sombra.

I had planned on taking her to Nuit. It is a three days' journey on foot. In my shadows, I could zip from Mavro to Nuit in no time, but Billie cannot join me in that form until she has my essence. Until then, I will stay as firm as she is. I won't bring her to the barracks in Mavro as that is no place for me to woo my mate, but I still have a home in Nuit that I am proud to show off to her.

Plus, Loki and his formerly mortal mate live in Nuit. My Billie might respond better to me if she has a human female to help explain what it means to be a Sombra demon's mate.

Gods know I didn't do a very good job of it.

But that will have to wait. If Duke Haures commands her presence, we will go. Together.

"Come, female," I say in English. I worry not about Vorn's reaction now. All of Sombra will know that I claim Billie as my mortal since I won't allow anyone to separate us. Not while I have her essence, but she doesn't yet have mine... or a bond to tie us together.

For a moment, I expect her to snap at me again. Or, worse, for her to shove off of my back and bolt.

But it seems as though she has learned her lesson.

"Where are we going?"

"To see Duke Haures."

CHAPTER 4
DUKE HAURES

BILLIE

It takes every ounce of media training I've ever had to keep from reacting when I meet this duke guy.

I thought he would look like my demon kidnapper. If not him, then the other demon who caught me. That one was all shadow, except for his green eyes. I could still make out some of his features, including his horns, and I'm sure he's definitely the same kind of demon as the first one.

Their duke? He looks nothing like them.

Well, no. That's not true. He has the same impressive height, the same linebacker-style build. He has horns, too, and fangs. His blue eyes glow, but they're so bright, they lend a bluish cast on the rest of him.

Because the rest of Duke Haures? Is pure *white*.

And I don't mean like caucasian white. I mean he doesn't have a drop of color to him except for his black claws and blue eyes.

He sits on a throne on top of a crystal dais. He has shadows behind him—more demons, I guess—and is in a room that is nothing like the outside of this world. The moon peering down on us through the gaps in the ceiling is blue, there are hovering balls of light the same coloring along the gold-accented wall, and it's much, much cooler.

I'm still in the demon world, though. Obviously. It was just my luck that, after the demon grabbed me, we landed in the ruler of Sombra's backyard.

In retrospect, I probably shouldn't have tried to take off on the demon I knew. If I hadn't gotten snagged almost immediately by another, who knows what other dangers I could've gotten into? I'm a stranger to this world. I don't know the rules. I have to be careful, and if that means following two demons through a vast field of smoke, fire, and shadows before arriving at the hidden oasis where the duke has his palace?

I will.

His name is Duke Haures. He introduces himself to me in English, and if I wasn't so taken aback by his appearance, the fact that he can speak my language would've done it. Do they all know English? My captor didn't at first, but then I took his hand to shake it—

foolishly believing he was offering me a truce—and then, wham!, we could communicate.

I didn't touch the duke, but that doesn't stop him from greeting me warmly to Sombra, his realm, and asking me how I know Glaine.

"Glaine?" I echo. "Who's Glaine?"

My demon kidnapper clears his throat. "I am Glaine."

"Well, how was I supposed to know that? We didn't have time for introductions before you *stole* me."

The demon duke steeples his claws. "Interesting. But he is your mate, yes?"

Mate? "What, like, lover? Partner? No! I just met the guy."

"But you called him to you."

Huh? "No."

"So it's true. It wasn't the *verus amor* spell that led him to you."

He's talking English, but I have no clue what he's talking *about*. "Um. I don't think so. I mean, he was just in my kitchen and, poof, now I'm here."

"You didn't open the *Grimoire du Sombra*?"

I shake my head.

"You didn't manifest Glaine to the human world?"

I give him a side-long look. "I had the weekend from hell, no offense meant. I was just heading to bed. I didn't manifest anything."

"Hmm."

"And, since I haven't, I'm sure you can see that this is one big mistake."

The duke nods, the magic light flashing off of his crystalline crown. "Yes, mortal. I agree with that."

As much as it rankles for this big demon ruler to call me 'mortal' like that, almost like he's dismissing me instead of being amazed to see a human woman, I keep my mouth shut. I just nod.

"And you're sure. You are not Glaine's mate."

Next to me, my demon kidnapper—Glaine—jerks in place. "Your grace—"

"No," I say firmly. "I'm not."

Duke Haures waves off to the side.

I don't know what that means, but the purple-eyed demon lurking in the shadows there nods.

As he drifts out toward me, I see that he wasn't just in the shadows. He *is* the shadows.

"Put your hands in front of you," commands the duke. "Now, mortal."

I have half a mind to refuse. What is he going to do to me if I do?

Second thought? I don't even want to imagine what these monsters will do if I piss them off. They have claws. Fangs. Holes on the outside that are filled with *fire*. And, yet, nothing seems more dangerous than this falsely regal demon with the crystalline crown.

Biting my tongue, I hold my hands out in front just like he ordered. The purple-eyed demon says something in that harsh demon language. The duke nods. The purple-eyed demon rubs his inky black hands together, and when he's done, he's conjured a length of golden chain between them, complete with thick manacles on each end.

He throws them at me. I flinch, bracing myself for the impact. It doesn't come, though when I move and hear metal clinking on metal, I glance down.

More magic, I guess. Because those chains? They're on *me*.

"Oh." The links span about two feet. I shake my hands, the rustling of the chains even louder in the stuffy throne room. "Oh, wow."

Oh, *no*.

Glaine frowns when he sees what's hanging off my wrists. "Duke Haures. Your grace. Chains? I don't think—"

"I have to," the duke responds, speaking in English again as he cuts Glaine off. So I can understand him? Or because I don't—but he wants to make sure I at least know that he has his reasons for putting me in these heavy, clunky things? "Remember what makes us shadow demons. If you can't follow—"

A muscle ticks in Glaine's solid cheek. Apart from the duke, he's the only other demon who isn't hovering in that strange shadowy version. "I'll burn," he supplies.

Wait. He'll *what*?

Duke Haures nods. "Yes. And where the mortal is going... you will stay behind in the throne room with me, Glaine. Do you understand?"

His gaze darts over to me. His nostrils flare, and he nods in return. "Of course, my lord."

"Very well. Vorn? If you would."

Vorn. The same green-eyed demon that found me after Glaine snarled, I panicked, and then I ran off, looking for a way out of here. He purposely avoids Glaine's glare as he gestures for me to follow him.

My feet are filthy. I'm covered in ash from my calves down, and my dress is sticking to my sweat-slicked skin. My curls are a droopy mess. It seems like a lifetime ago that I fueled up on caffeine, but those three espressos are kicking my ass right now. I'm annoyed and worried and, damn it, a little bit scared—and I cover that up by jutting out my chin and sticking my nose in the air while my mind runs a mile a minute, searching for a way out of this mess.

Or, at the very least, a bathroom.

No such luck.

What are they going to do to me? Well, how about putting me in a pair of golden chains, then leading me underground to a damp, chilly *dungeon*?

Because that's where I am. At least four flights

below the throne room where I left Duke Haures, Glaine, and the other demons, I'm led by a pair of green-eyed guards who flank me the entire way to the cell. I don't know what kind of danger they think I am. I'm half their size and wearing chains... but they're not taking any chances. They march me in silence before leaving me behind in a dank, chilly cell about the size of my bathroom at home.

I don't look around. Beyond a basin that might be a sink and a cot, there's not much else here. I'm hoping like hell that the sink isn't a demon version of a toilet because... yeah, that's not gonna be fun. Instead, I drop down on the cot, letting it hit me that, yeah... this is really happening.

I don't panic. What will that do? I'm a problem-solver.

This is just a much bigger problem than I'm used to.

Maybe I need sleep. If I'm lucky, this will turn out to be a stress-induced nightmare. With all the adrenaline that's been pumping through me since I realized I was abducted by a demon, I've burned off the last of those espressos. If I can't pee, eat, or wash this gunk off my legs, I might as well sleep and look at this problem with a fresh pair of eyes tomorrow.

No, it's not hiding from my problems. It's recharging to figure them out tomorrow.

And I'm halfway to convincing myself I actually

believe that bullshit when I hear heavy steps plodding down the stairs again.

I perk up.

Was it a mistake?

Did they realize I'm not supposed to be here?

Are they coming to take me home?

I rise up from the cot, then exhale roughly when I see a shadowy purple-eyed guard—and Glaine.

It has to be him. The scowl that was on his face as I was led out of the throne room is still there, and he's the only other demon I've seen in his solid form other than Duke Haures. Who knows? Maybe he's the weird-looking one, not the duke...

No. The guy sat on the throne like he was daring someone to say something about his appearance. Glaine must be what the other demons look like when they're not being pitch-black shadows with glowing eyes instead of the duke.

I blink. What the... why am I worried about this? Especially when the purple-eyed demon uses a key to open the cell, then marches in with Glaine.

I glare at him. "What are you doing here?"

He shakes his head, long hair swaying. At the purple-eyed demon's nod, Glaine lifts his hands in front of him. The other demon does that conjuring thing again, but instead of throwing chains at him, he closes his fists and jerks his hand.

Both Glaine and I follow the motion, both of our

bodies moving with his. When he's done, I'm still wearing one half of the chain. Glaine has the other manacled to his wrist.

We're connected by the same length.

Once he's done his job, the other demon leaves, slamming the cell door closed behind him.

I immediately turn my ire on Glaine.

I don't feel bad that he's down here with me. This is his fault, and I'm being *more* punished by being locked in a small cell with the demon who stole me.

So, again, I demand, "What are you doing here?"

"I asked Duke Haures if I could go to the dungeon in your stead. He pointed out that you could only be released if you are a Sombra demon's mate, otherwise you're in breach of his first law. You said it yourself," he adds, and though he'd kept his tone flat and emotionless when he first started talking, it cracks a little at that part. "You're not my mate. You've denied me. The consequence of that is you are a rogue human who knows about Sombra. That's not allowed. Until he decides what to do with you, you'll stay in the dungeon."

That explains me. And while I don't like that explanation, I get it. I can work with that. There's gotta be a way out.

But what about him?

"Let me guess: you got tossed in here because you kidnapped a human. Right?"

"No. I did what I thought was right, and Duke Haures understands why I did it. But whether you deny me or not, you are my mate, mortal. And I will be by your side until you accept that."

Considering the chains attaching us together, he means that literally.

"Bullshit."

"Pardon?"

"You heard me. I said bullshit. You don't just get to pick your mate—"

"You are correct. I didn't. The gods gave you to me." I want to call bullshit again, but before I do, he continues. "Sombra demons get one true mate. Their fated mate. We wait as long as it takes... decades in the human world, centuries, millennia... however long it takes to find our mate or have our female call us to her. You are mine."

No, I'm not.

"Let me say this plainly so we both know where we stand: humans have this little thing called 'free will'. We can pick and choose our partners"—and have them use us because they're obsessed with another woman—"and change them whenever we want. You get one mate. I could have five husbands." I pause. "Well, not at the same time. That's polygamy, and while poly couples are cool, I've always been a monogamous chick."

All the more reason why Trevor pissed me off when

he said that he needed to be with Whiskey like he needed air, but to show that he didn't consider his year with me wasted, he'd pity-bang me whenever I got horny.

Yeah. No, thanks. I'd rather take a ride with a demon—

I shake my head. "Anyway, my point stands. Humans don't have mates."

"Perhaps not," Glaine says. "But they can be a demon's mate."

I'm sure they can. He seems pretty human-ish. He has two hands. Two legs. Two feet that, while his nails are definitely closer to claws, aren't cloven hooves. No tail, and the horns are actually more intriguing to me than they have any right to be. If he has a penis, I'm sure we could *technically* mate—because, yup, I'm under no illusion that what he wants is to get laid— though here's hoping he's on the smaller side for his build because, otherwise, I don't see how his tab A would ever fit in my slot B—

Oh my God. Am I really thinking about the logistics of fucking a demon?

"It's impossible. This... it can't be happening. I mean, look at me. I'm not a demon. I'm a *human*. We can't be mates!"

I can't be his mate!

"Of course you can."

He's not listening. I can't say he's not looking since

he hasn't taken his eyes off of me yet, but he doesn't get it. "Glaine—"

My first impression of the demon was that he is big. My second is that he is stoic, yet grumpy. My third is that he is a guy used to getting his way.

That doesn't change as he looks down his long nose at me and says flatly, "You're not the first to be joined to one of my kind."

BILLIE

Looking back on it, that was probably the most obvious thing in the world. If not that other humans, like, *married* demons or something, then that they've been to Earth before. If they're such a big secret that people are sent to the *dungeon* to protect that secret, it would explain why it's never got out to the press before.

I respect that.

I don't like it. But I respect it.

And then Glaine goes on to say, "There is a reason I was in your apartment when I found you, Billie."

Oh, really? I've got to hear this.

"There's a book. The *Grimoire du Sombra*. It's a spell book full of magic. Human magic. If a human reads the *verus amor*... the 'true love' spell... and they're fated to be the mate to one of my kind, we are summoned. Manifested. I didn't go to your world tonight because you summoned me, though if I had been more patient I'm sure you would have. I went to your world in search of the book."

"Cool story, but we don't have that book. Trust me. I live in our study when I'm home, and know all the books we have on the shelves. There's no spell book."

"There was," insists Glaine. "And I know that because a Sombra demon was summoned to your quarters by that spell recently. It wasn't the book that called me to your home. It was his essence. His, and that of the female who is his mate."

Okay. This isn't funny anymore. "Forget it."

He doesn't.

"I believe the demon who was summoned to your quarters is the mate to your kin." He scrunches his face. "Sierra."

He's gone too far now.

"How do you know about Sierra?" I demand.

Any hint of arrogance that was in his stance before as he *told* me I was supposed to be his mate disappears, swallowed up by his obvious confusion. "I have your essence. I know that she is your kin, and that you are very fond of her. But I also know that, before I met you, she must've met Dagon and now she is his mate."

Forget that second part for a second. "You have my *what*?"

"Your essence," he says again. He uses his claws to gesture at his bare chest. "That what makes Billie Billie. Your emotions. Your memories. Your hopes. *You.*"

"You mean like my soul?" Are you serious? "You took my soul, too?"

"When you touched my hand—"

That didn't answer my question. "You stole my soul?"

"I accepted your essence so that I would know you. So I could speak in your human language with you. So that I could help you understand your fate."

My fate? My fate is to watch Sierra become the next Madonna.

But, wait—

"You took mine. If I take your soul—"

"My essence."

Sure. "Whatever. If you pass it to me... I'll know everything about your world?"

"You have to accept it."

He said something like that before. "Accept it' implies that it's a gift being given, right? But I didn't give you mine."

Glaine smirks. I have half a mind to take off my shoe and whip it at him to get that smirk off his face, but I don't have a shoe. And I probably would miss, considering he's so much taller than me. Still. I'm even more annoyed.

"You didn't know how to guard it. I'll take anything you have to offer me, female—"

I meet his smirk with a scowl of my own. "You have my essence. You know my name. Use it, okay?"

His smirk wavers, and I see a hopeful light in his eyes before he purposely extinguishes it. "And I have your permission to address you so familiarly?"

"You have my permission to pull that stick out of your ass," I say sweetly.

Glaine frowns. "There is no wood in my behind, mortal. That is not something we do in Sombra."

I roll my eyes. "It's an expression. Never mind. It's not worth it. But, listen... calling me 'female' or 'mortal' or... or 'human'... that's degrading, okay? It's like calling you 'demon'. Would you like that?"

"You may call me anything you wish so long as it's yours." A touch of sudden humor... and maybe lust... softens his harsh features. "Your mate. Your male." Oh, yeah. That's definitely lust now as he just about purrs, "Your lover."

"I'll stick with Glaine, thanks."

Hey. It's better than calling him my kidnapper.

"As you wish."

I roll my eyes, letting what he told me about the essence-thing mull around my head for a second.

I'm pretty sure the duke took pity on me and spoke

in English. And while I'm curious and want to know how the ruler of this demon world learned a human language, that's on the back burner for now. My big concern is that no one else seems to know it. I'm surrounded by a world full of giant demons who can all talk about me, chained to the one who abducted me because 'fate told him to' or some nonsense like that, and I have to rely on him translating Sombran to English for me—plus trust that he's not making it all up if it's something I wouldn't like to hear.

I could let him give me his essence. His soul. I'd know everything about him... and if that sounds too good to be true, that's because it most likely is.

"What's the fine print?"

Like every other time I say something that might not have a direct translation in his language, Glaine furrows his brow, making his ridges stand out. "I do not understand."

I figured. "The fine print is kind of like a small warning that's not as obvious from the beginning. Like, I say that I'll accept your essence, but there's something I don't know about how that'll affect me unless I look for the fine print, or I ask."

I'm in show business. Sierra's lawyers are essential to making sure she gets a fair deal on every one of her contracts, but I don't let Charlotte and her team go through them until I've read the mumbo jumbo and the legalese first.

Glaine thinks it over for a moment, then admits, "I have your essence. If you accept mine from me, that is the first step to finalizing our mate bond."

Right. This mate bond that he's certain exists, but that I'm having a hard time buying. He really wants me to believe that demons get a fated mate, just one, and that he's so sure that I'm his, he's willing to do the demon version of marriage with me? And, unless I've gotten it wrong, there's no way out. No divorces. No annulments. It's a true 'til death do we part' situation, only how does that work when demons are immortal?

I shake my head. Logically, I can't accept that I'm fated to be mystically bonded to a demon from another realm. I *can't*. Not even if, the more I'm looking at him, the more... *human* it seems to me. He's not just a demon. He's Glaine, my kidnapper, and the big guy who willingly offered to join me in the cell so I wouldn't be alone.

Not that his motives are entirely altruistic. Whether I am his mate or not, that doesn't change the fact that he *believes* I am. Having me chained to him puts me right where he wants me: with him. It'll be a lot easier for him to go ahead with his demon courtship if I'm here instead of back on Earth or wandering by myself in the demon world.

"That's never going to happen," I tell him bluntly.

He seems to disagree.

"I will do whatever I must to show you that I will be

a good and honorable and devoted mate to you. Ask for anything in my power, female, and it is yours."

There's such a weight to his promise that I immediately feel like I'm buckling beneath it. I want to shrug it off, push past it, but the fact that it makes me so uncomfortable just slams home the realization that I'm in a dungeon with a seven-foot-tall demon, wearing little more than a skimpy red dress and my underwear, my feet are filthy, I'm feeling the effects from the coffee I downed and the no sleep I've gotten, and somewhere in a world out of my reach, Sierra is probably waking up, wondering where the hell I am.

Oh, and I don't have my phone. I've never felt so goddamn naked and unprepared in my life as I do in this situation, and my determination that there isn't anything I can't do if I put my mind to it is really beginning to waver right about now.

"I told you," I mutter. "My name is Billie."

"Billie," he says solemnly. "Tell me. I will do it."

He wants to know? Fine.

"Help me get out of here. Help me get home."

When he doesn't respond to my conditions, I snort.

That's what I thought.

DO YOU KNOW HOW HARD IT IS TO IGNORE SOMEONE when you're chained to them?

The answer is: *very.*

Glaine is so big that he takes up half the cell just by himself. And maybe that's a bit of an exaggeration. He's definitely gotta be pushing seven feet—maybe more if you count the horns—and he's two, maybe three times as wide as me. It doesn't matter that he's crouching low to the hard, chilled floor, leaving the narrow cot for me. He looms, even with his back to me, and his silence is suffocating.

The clinking of the chain whenever each of us moves is about as much noise as I pick up. My professional side can't help but be impressed by the dungeon's excellent soundproofing. I guess the duke doesn't want to be bothered by his prisoners' misery—and, for the moment at least, only Glaine and I are locked up down here—which means that there is nothing to distract me from my cellmate.

So I find a way to distract myself. After complaining about how the ash turned my legs grey, I start to explore the sink-thing. Turns out, it is a sink. He shows me how to use it, and since it's similar to motion-sensor sinks back home, it's easy.

Using the toilet... not so much.

There's a hole in one corner, so dark I didn't notice it at first. About the size of a dinner plate, it seems bottomless. Two smaller holes are positioned next to it. When I finally can't hold it any longer—those damn espressos doing a number on my bladder—I ask Glaine what I'm supposed to do.

That's how I discover that, in Sombra, you squat over the hole to go to the bathroom, then shift over to the other two. One is air. One is water. A mystical bidet that gets the job done if you're not shy.

Luckily, I'm not.

As if eager to prove that he's also a gentlemanly demon, Glaine gives me his back while I do my business. I clean up as best I can, using the sink to rinse off my hands, then clink my way back to the cot.

He says nothing at all as I curl up on top of it, facing away from him. Smart demon. One wrong word and I'm primed to explode. I need sleep. Now that I've accepted there is no getting rid of him—and after a questionable meal of hot meat and something that could pass for human potatoes brought down to us by a guard—I'm not fighting my growing unconsciousness any longer.

It's only as I start to drift off that I hear his deep voice from somewhere behind me.

"I will sit at your feet, my mate. I will watch over you. Have no fear while your male is near."

I'm too tired to tell him I'm not afraid, I'm pissed. Or to remind him that he's not my male. Instead, I make a non-committal sound that suggests I couldn't care less what he does before I fall asleep, hoping like hell that, back in the human world, Sierra and Three still haven't figured out I'm missing yet...

CHAPTER 6

HARTH

GLAINE

My mate is asleep, and as I vowed to her, I am watching over her as she slumbers.

She makes a soft humming sort of noise as she curls up on her side, giving her back to me. The golden ringlets—*curls*, I amend as a sense of pride... Billie's pride... filters into my consciousness— are pillowed beneath her cheek. So is the hand not attached to a manacle. Duke Haures is merciful enough to have a small cot in his dungeon cells, but humans are a lot less sturdy than we demons. She needs comfort, but she doesn't trust me enough to provide it.

The most she allows is for me to gather up the length of chain, sitting on the floor beside the cot. The chain is long enough that, if she ordered me to the other side of the cell, it would stretch, but she didn't. Instead, murmuring something about a creature she calls 'Three', she shrugged when I suggested boldly that I watch over her from a closer distance.

Delving into her essence, I see that this 'Three' is not unlike one of the ungez, the prey beasts that live in the shadows. Though it is an Earth beast, it appears to be made up of shadows like so many Sombran creatures, with eyes that shine the same color as mine even if they don't glow. She tends to it like it is her spawn, feeding and brushing and protecting the not-ungez, and I find myself jealous of a creature that has both my mate's affection and attention while I have none.

As she snuffles, I wonder if, perhaps, this creature is a guide to earning both for myself. She thinks that I am like her 'void' when I drop my big body into a crouch beside her, watching her studiously. Using her memories, I see if there are other ways I can mimic the wee beast. It does not speak in anything other than soft yowls, and it seems as though its hours are spent sleeping and licking its genitals.

Sombra demons rarely require much sleep; a testament to how I can guard for cycles at a time without tiring, and will do so gladly now that I have a mate to watch over. As for feeling a tongue on my cock... Billie's essence says that is also done to males in her world, but usually by their female mates.

Even in my shadows, I am not flexible enough to taste my own cock. I never would've thought such a thing possible, but the idea of my mortal mate opening her pretty mouth and feeling her cold breath on my hard flesh... it's all I can do not to spill seed on the floor of our shared cell.

Until Billie has accepted me as her mate—until she has accepted my essence—I cannot hope for her to pleasure me in such a way. And though I can sense that she's done it to other males, I firmly stop those memories of hers from surfacing in my mind. I already despise this Trevor, both for causing Billie pain and for not recognizing that she was the best female he could ever have. His loss, and I would've claimed Billie as my one true mate even if she still felt fondness for that male.

But she does not. That means her heart is free to be earned, and now that I understand that humans don't feel the mate bond instinctively... that they only do once they've developed fondness for their fated demon... I must change the way I approach wooing her.

First? I can't do so in the dungeons.

Second? My Billie is a proud, fierce female. She will only dislike me further if she continues to feel like she has no say in things. I thought that, by bringing her to Sombra, I could show her that she was meant to be with her male in his realm. That was a mistake. She needed to choose to follow me here, but in my own stubborn need, I took that choice from her.

Just like Duke Haures took her freedom to completely deny me again...

I won't say that I regret what I've done. I only rue the fact that I've hurt her, and make the same vow to myself that I did to Billie before: that I will do anything to prove to her that I am worthy to be her male.

And that begins with breaking her out of the dungeon.

The one plus to having served Duke Haures for centuries? I know how the male thinks. I can gauge his moods, and tell when he will show mercy to a prisoner. He would've kept me out of the dungeon if I hadn't requested to be placed with Billie; of course, separating me from my mate would've been a harsher punishment, a fact he knows very well. That he allowed me to join her, even going so far as to command that we wear the chains together... Duke Haures is doing what is expected of him as ruler, while also giving me the chance to woo my mate.

Will he be furious that I plan to leave the dungeon with Billie? I think he will, but I also doubt that he'll consider it a shadow offense. He won't end my existence, not when I only did what I did because I was shocked to find my fated mate.

If any demon in Sombra knows what it's like to make mistakes because he learned his mate was a human of legend, it's Duke Haures. That is the only reason why I concoct my plan. Not because I would betray his grace, but because I know that he would almost expect it of *me*.

As the head of the guard, I've handpicked and trained nearly every single soldier who serves Duke Haures. Of course, he has their complete loyalty, but so do I. He is their monarch; I am their captain. Duke Haures must be obeyed, but after decades of training before they're given their own posts or commands, it is ingrained into every green-eyed soldier to do as they're told by their superior soldier.

In Mavro, there is no guard that has a higher rank than I do. For centuries, I've led Duke Haures's personal guard, and there isn't a demon who serves in the palace who doesn't owe that fact to my training them.

Still, I must choose carefully. I know that, whatever guard is given the task to check on their former commander in the cells, it will be one who shares some loyalty to me. Again, I know my reputation. I am a hard taskmaster. I've been called cocky. Arrogant. Heartless. After Lilith, that was true.

But I have Billie now. And, for her sake, I hope that the next guard that comes to stroll by the cell is one that I can put the trust of her mortal existence into.

The dungeons are impenetrable. Even if they weren't, the enchanted chains steal much of my power.

I cannot shift to my shadows or slip through the bars while wearing them. With Billie chained to me, I'm even more hampered. The guards have no reason to patrol down here unless they're curious, or they're bringing our next meal. There is nothing for me to do except wait.

Hours pass. I don't mind them so much because keeping watch over Billie... I'm more at peace than I have been in the last few centuries. I am eager to prove myself, yes, but also determined to let her rest.

And then, just when I begin to wonder if Duke Haures will skip our next meal, I hear heavy steps on the stairs leading down into the dungeon. I hold my breath, rising up from my crouch so that I can greet the other guard as a proud male would, while still protecting my mate.

The younger male has corkscrew horns, dark green eyes, and is carrying a tray between his claws. I recognize his flatter nose, his shorter hair, and his hesitancy to approach a superior guard—and I grin.

As though I needed the push to put my plan into motion. Seeing Harth be the guard that Duke Haures sent down to the dungeon... my most recent recruit, and the demon who looks up to me as a father figure... knowing that he is too inexperienced to be a match to a wily, older demon... I thank you, your grace. Duke Haures has sent me my freedom without giving me the key.

But that is alright.

Harth has one on his belt.

Moving toward the bars, I give the younger demon a welcoming grin. "Ah. Harth. Just the demon I was hoping to see…"

CHAPTER 7
JAILBREAK

BILLIE

As I slowly respond to the gentle shake on my shoulder, my half-asleep and still exhausted brain tells me that I'm waking up. Good thing, too.

I just had the weirdest nightmare.

I don't know what part of it was worse: how Trevor sat me down and told me that he was secretly in love with Sierra, or how I left his sorry behind back in Connecticut, drove home to Manhattan in a pair of three-inch stiletto heels, only to let myself into our quiet apartment and get *kidnapped* by a *shadow demon*.

To make matters worse, the giant demon broke his race's biggest rule by bringing me here and revealing the existence of demons and alternate dimensions when humans aren't allowed to know about them. Of course, if I was his fated mate—the one female destined to, like, marry him and have his half-human, half-demon babies—then it would be okay. I'd be expected to keep my demon hubby's secrets. But since I'm just regular old Billie Bickles and I'm *not* a demon's one true mate, then I'm kinda screwed.

Luckily, it's just one hell of a vivid dream. I mean, I always had a bit of an imagination, and if I were a writer instead of Sierra's manager, it would make a pretty good idea for a book, but it's not real. It can't be.

Tell that to the male with the fangs, ridges over his nose, and gleaming black horns who has no concept of personal space.

My eyes blink open, expecting to find Sierra right there, ready to convince me that she's moved on from worrying about Patrick Ridgefield, her throat feels fine, and I can put an end to the vocal rest her doctor put her on. It wouldn't work, especially since she's been attempting something similar for the last week, but I'll give my friend credit for her persistence—and for only throwing a small tantrum when I give her a look and she knows better to drop it.

But that's not Sierra. The ends of his thick black hair tickle my nose as I subconsciously turn toward him, but the second my brain wakes up fully and I see

Glaine staring down at me, the rest of me jolts back into consciousness.

Right. Because it wasn't a dream. I really am in the bowels of a palace, locked in the dungeon because I was too proud to act like I might possibly be Glaine's mate. To make matters worse, we've been chained together, and while I warned him not to sneak his way onto the cot with me—as if his big, muscular body could fit—he's so tall that, kneeling on the floor, he can still loom over me.

I jolt, and his reflexes have him backing away before I can accidentally bash my forehead into the killer points on his horns. My heart's thundering in my chest. Scowling at the demon, I rub my boobs, the scowl only deepening when his gaze drops, eying up my cleavage.

"Stop that," I tell him, and there's less heat in my voice than there was earlier tonight. Spitfire Billie is taking a backseat for the moment. Professional Billie is still looking for a loophole to get me out of this mess, while Billie herself is too tired for this bullshit.

I'm stuck here. The clanking of the chains as I move my hand is a reminder of that. I'm stuck with Glaine. I have to make the best of a bad situation, and on the plus side, at least I know what it is that he wants: *me.* Meanwhile, I just want to go home.

Let's see which one of us gets what they want first.

I glare at Glaine. His glowing eyes dim a little, but

his gaze lifts so that he's meeting mine. "Did you sleep enough?"

He doesn't apologize. I'm beginning to think he's allergic to it. Whatever. Like I said, guys are guys no matter what world they come from. It doesn't help that this dress came with a built-in bra so I don't have anything to cover my tits and, whoops, the fabric must've shimmied down while I was knocked out. I haven't burst out of the top, but there's more than enough cleavage on display that I can't really blame Glaine for getting distracted. He's made it clear from the get-go that he's attracted to me, and if he doesn't look as monstrous as I remember, I blame that on still being a little dozy.

Besides, he gave me the perfect excuse to avoid his probing stare.

Grabbing the top of my dress, yanking it up so that my nips are firmly tucked inside of the crappy bra, I purposely look at a point over his shoulder. Oh, wow. The toilet hole is just as fascinating as it was last night...

He continues to stare. In fact, he rarely blinks at all, as though he doesn't want to miss a split second of watching his mate's face.

I'd be flattered if I wasn't so determined to prove that he was *wrong*.

"Did I get enough sleep? Please. After the night I had, I need more than a couple of hours to sleep it off.

And since we're stuck in this cell for the time being, plus I don't have my phone to cancel any of the *many* appointments I'm probably missing, getting some more sleep seems like a much better idea."

I keep my voice short. Clipped. *Professional.* There's no-nonsense in the tone, and if I offended Glaine by implying that I'd prefer nodding off to dreamland than sitting here while he stares at me, well... I'm not implying anything. I'll say it to his face and probably just get another grumpy glower for my trouble.

"Very well," Glaine says, nodding solemnly. "I had thought you'd rather leave the dungeon cell and see more of Sombra, but if you like the cot..."

Hang on.

My head snaps to my left. I stopped paying attention to the closed cell door after that other green-eyed demon closed it behind Glaine. It was a reminder that I was trapped, and while I'm not all that claustrophobic, the closed door made it clear that I couldn't just get up and go whenever I wanted to.

That's my problem. I know I'm privileged. I grew up poor, and in a lot of ways I still have that same mentality even after all the success I've found; first with Thr33peat, then as Sierra's manager. That doesn't make me any less privileged, though it gives me a better grasp on what I have and what I can lose. My freedom is the biggest one I have. Money helps. Without money, I couldn't go where I want, when I want. The fact that I'm a pretty white woman is up there. I'm slender. I have my health. I do well because I'm tenacious, but I never forget that there are women just like me who could make demands and get laughed at. I snap my fingers, usually in Sierra's name, and the world is my oyster.

On Earth, though. Being dragged to Sombra is a reality check. I have no power here. I have to rely on Glaine, and with the two of us trapped in this cell, I can do so without having to play into his belief that I'm his mate. He's stuck, too, whether he chose to be or not. He could ignore me if he wanted to, but since he obviously wants to make a good impression on me, I doubt he will.

That doesn't mean I appreciated the reminder that I'm completely at his mercy, and that of the pale demon duke upstairs. Looking at the closed door... I haven't hit one day locked in this cell. I'd go nuts if I didn't stubbornly pretend that I could leave whenever I choose to.

So I've been ignoring it, even going so far as to turn my back on it while I struggled to fall asleep. It was better to stare at the wall than admit I'm stuck on my own, far from where Sierra and Three and even our head of security and years-long father figure, Roy, have any idea where I am. They're probably looking for me right now, and all I want is to find a way back to them—

—and that begins by getting the hell out of the dungeon.

Which I can. Because the cell door?

It's *open.*

"How?" I breathe out. Is it a trap? Something tells me that it might be, but without Glaine's essence, I don't know for sure. I honestly don't care, either. I ask, but I'm barely listening as he explains that he called in a favor from a fellow guard to 'forget' to close the door behind him before he scampered off.

Sure, he doesn't say it quite like that. His English is a lot more stilted and formal, probably because, as a language, so is Sombran. I get the gist, though, and he could've told me that Duke Haures opened the door himself because he realized he made a mistake, and I would've accepted such a whopper just to get the hell out of here.

Glaine will have to come with me. He promises that our next step will be to find a mage who can take these chains off of us, but unless I want to gnaw off my own hand to lose him, I'm having company on my jailbreak.

I don't argue. I wouldn't even if I could. He made a very valid point earlier that I won't fit into his world without his essence. Refusing his offer to share it with me might be a mistake, but I don't like the idea of not knowing quite what it'll cost me to say 'yes'. With

Glaine right there with me, he can help me survive this world.

Besides, he asked me what I wanted from him to prove himself. *Help me get out of here. Help me get home.* Maybe he feels bad for upending my life the way he did. Maybe this is his way of making amends.

And maybe I'm hoping the demon is a good guy because he's the only hope I have to get back to New York...

The guards take sporadic tours through the dungeon. We're meant to have two meals a day, one that's like breakfast, one that's dinner, and I slept for an indeterminable amount of time. I don't know how long it's been since Glaine's guard buddy agreed to leave the door open, only that he'd come with the breakfast meal when he did. I see it on the tray on the ground behind Glaine, the unfamiliar meat we ate last night still steaming.

So not long then. Glaine probably waited for the guard to disappear, giving him plausible deniability, then started to shake me awake.

I'm up now. Excited about the prospect of getting out, but the way my stomach aches... yeah. I'm hungry, too. Scooting off the bed, Glaine's eyes watching my every move, I use the napkin on the tray to wrap up the meat. I'm taking my meal to-go.

Glaine nods approvingly. "We can eat as we travel," he says. "But we must hurry. Harth only promised that he'd keep the back hall clear until the next guard takes his patrol."

I don't know how long that is, but as one of the duke's guards, he does. If he thinks we must hurry, it can't be that long.

"I'm ready when you are," I tell him.

For a moment, he seems stunned that I'm not arguing. That I'm not trying to come up with a way to leave him behind. Please. Give up my guide through Sombra who has a selfish reason to keep me safe? Even without the chains keeping us together, I learned my lesson. Until I'm home again, I'm trusting him to watch over me the same way he did while I was asleep.

It isn't often I trust others, Sierra and Roy excluded. Anytime I finally let down my guard, like I did with Trevor, it tends to bite me in the ass. I have no reason to believe that Glaine won't be another Trevor—despite the fact that he seems to want *me* as his mate—but I have no choice other than to hope he wants to get laid bad enough that he'll help bring me back home.

Am I above trading sex to get what I want? Right now, not even a little. I won't go there if I don't have to. It's not fair to either of us, not when I'm sure I'm not his mate and Glaine's sure I *am*, but if a little nookie gets me back home before Sierra discovers that I'm in trouble... hey. He's not looking so bad at the moment, and I can only imagine how he might become more attractive the longer I know him.

It's my turn to stare at him now. Can he tell what I'm thinking? I know my essence gave him access to English, my name, and my memories... but the way his expression has turned heated, his eyes glowing impossibly brighter as he starts to inch his way closer to me...

I dart around him before he can get too closer. In a heartbeat, I'm standing outside of the cell while Glaine is dabbing his bottom lip with his tongue, reaching up to stroke his right horn with his free hand.

"Billie..."

The way he groans my name is a plea. If I had any doubt that he's attracted to me, or that he sensed that fleeting yet charged moment between us, they're *gone*.

Crap. I'm playing a dangerous game with this demon, but what else can I do? He *stole* me. I want to go home—and I'll do whatever I have to to make sure I do.

His voice is a plea. Mine? It's a hint of a tease as I tug on the chain, gesturing for him to join me outside the cell. "Come on. What are you waiting for?"

Glaine doesn't hesitate. Leaving the half-touched tray behind him, he's by my side in seconds. He shudders, then straightens, as if putting his obvious arousal away for the moment. "This way," he rumbles. "If we go down that hall, we can leave the palace without Duke Haures realizing we've left."

I fall into step behind him. The chain won't let me get too far from him, but I'm not taking any chances.

Keeping my voice low, I ask, "Won't the duke be pissed you're helping me escape?"

"It doesn't matter what his grace thinks of me." His glowing green eyes slide my way again. It's like he can't keep them off of me for long. "He is not my mate."

Yeah? Well, neither am I.

Right?

BILLIE

I don't know what happened while I was sleeping. If my demon kidnapper grew a conscience or he finally caught on to the fact that you can't just steal a woman, proclaim her as your mate because 'fate said' blah-blah-blah, and expect she's going to just go along with it... it doesn't matter. I told him I wanted out of the dungeon and, poof, he found a way to get us out.

Now, do I believe he did this out of the kindness of his heart? Yeah, right. Trevor broke me the other night almost easily as I snapped my stiletto heel. I've got the business acumen all right, but I've never been suspicious to a fault until I got grabbed by the guard.

In a way, Glaine also broke me a bit. When he obviously has ulterior motives that only make sense to the demons of this hellish world, I can't put anything past him. Did he really call in a favor with one of the guards he knows? Or is this all some long con? Who knows? Maybe he had a key or something, just waiting for me to knock out so he could put his plan into motion. Then he could wake me up and, look at that, play the hero as he helps me out of the dungeon.

It could've happened like that. Then again, he could be telling me the truth. There's no way to know. I always thought I was an amazing judge of character. I mean, I knew Jared Turner was a dick back when I met him and he was barely seventeen. I've saved Sierra from signing more bad deals than I can count because something didn't sit right with me. I liked to think I can trust my gut—

—and then Trevor Daniels fooled me for way longer than he should've been able to. I didn't even love the guy. We had fun and he was one hell of an actor since I really thought he cared about me, but I was already set to dump him before he made it clear that, while he might've cared, he didn't love me the way he loved Whiskey Rose.

He blindsided me. Now that the worst of the shock has worn off, I can admit that. The first time he asked me about Sierra possibly receiving certain fan letters last week, it barely pinged my overprotective meter. I left him open to make a move on her, and worse? Now that I'm trapped in this demon world, I can't even warn her about Trevor.

Not like I think he's going to go right after her. I made it clear that, as soon as I arrived back in Manhattan, I was letting her know to stay away from him. I told *him* to stay away from her. I'm kicking myself now—and have been since I've been stuck in Sombra—that I didn't go straight to Sierra's room last night to tell her instead of wimping out and heading to the kitchen instead.

What kind of bestie am I? What kind of *manager*? She's my client, plus the closest thing to a sister I have. I'll never forgive myself if anything happens to her—if Trevor turns out to be another Patrick Ridgefield after all—and I couldn't stop it because Glaine decided to take me home with him.

I get it. Kinda. If I was given a fated mate who was meant for me, loved *me*, and would never cheat... wouldn't I want to grab onto them and hold tight? But that's how it works for demons, not humans, and no amount of telling him otherwise is going to change his mind.

That's okay. He wants to pretend I'm his mate? Go right ahead. If he wants to loop up the excess chain keeping us connected so that it doesn't drag and I don't trip? Anything to get us out of the dungeon faster. He takes the lead, warning me back as he vows in that deep voice of his that he won't let anything get me?

I hang back, because while I might be independent, I'm not an idiot. I've traveled all over the world. I know there are customs and unsaid expectations for locals, and if the fact that I'm *human* won't mark me as the most obvious tourist ever, the chains that belong to a *fugitive* make everything worse.

When we first landed in this world... in Sombra... all I saw were smoke and ash and fire. To be fair, I was more concerned with turning around and running right back to New York to care that I was in a literal Hell. Not even being mean, either. The air is scorching, the rotten egg stink is overwhelming, and there are *demons* everywhere I go. And not just regular Lucifer-type demons, either. Glaine's red skin and black horns are devilish, but that other guard I met was nothing but *shadows*.

Duh. They're shadow demons, right? They can swap from one form to another instinctively, going somewhat transparent as they hide in the shadows that make up this world, but lucky me: the gold chains aren't just an accessory or a way to mark us as prisoners. They're charmed to contain Glaine's powers. He's stuck as a demon.

The chains do nothing to me except annoy me. I'm a human, and my power revolves around scheduling all of the demands on a pop star's time without double-booking. The chains are just heavy and slow me down while keeping me connected to my unrepentant kidnapper who you'd think would be a lot happier that we broke out of the dungeon without anyone seeing us.

Then again, maybe not. Glaine glances over his shoulders repeatedly as he guides me outside. Me? I enjoy the slight freshness that comes with the blue-tinged sky, knowing that once we leave the oasis surrounding the duke's palace, we're heading right back to the black shadows, reddish ash, and the stink.

It's no better the second time. My poor feet are filthy in mere steps, and once again I wish I'd had the foresight to throw on some slippers before getting *captured*.

Still, I'm a trooper. I'm also a firm believer in the saying: 'better the devil you know'. Glaine's proven to me—so far—that he has a vested interest in keeping me out of danger. Even without the chain, I'd stick by him since I need the tour guide.

Not like he's showing off his realm. As soon as we put enough distance between us and the palace, he relaxes a little, but he pushes me to move faster.

Does he think I want to spend the rest of my life in a dungeon in Hell? Please. I can't work toward going home behind bars. I'm trying, but the ash is difficult to navigate without shoes, and I can hardly match his pace even without the expectant way he glowers at me whenever I stumble.

"Maybe the next time you decide to kidnap a

human, pick one who's dressed for escape," I snap, sick of it. "Sorry that I left my leggings and sneakers behind when you, oh, yeah, *stole* me."

If there's one thing I'm going to do, it's hold a grudge. He decided he could take me because I was his? Well, he's going to see that side of Billie as I never let him forget for a second.

What's he going to do? Leave me behind in the shadows? We're chained together, and though he promises that that's our next step—that he's bringing me to someone who knows how to remove those chains, and who should do it if Glaine asks—we haven't been able to separate just yet.

Only one problem with that plan. Glaine admitted that, in his demon form, the demon city we're going to is *three* days' walk away from the capital. Three days. In this skintight red dress that is constantly riding up. Three days in no shoes. Three days where I'm not sure how I'm going to eat, where I'm going to sleep, and if I'm going to make it without dropping to the ash and telling the big demon to just leave me behind.

He won't. It doesn't take long to realize that. Glaine is as stubborn as I am because, after the first time I do stumble and trip, landing on my knees in the ash, he's there to swoop me up in his arms.

"It will be faster this way," he rumbles.

"Put me down." I slap his bicep. "You're not carrying me for the next three days."

"Why not?" he asks, and I can somehow sense his confusion. "I am a strong male, and you are a wee mortal. Your hair may be big and as pretty as the rest of my mate, but it doesn't add weight if that is your concern."

I sputter. "It's not my curls that make me heavy, *demon*." Hey. If I'm back to being a mortal, he can be a demon. "It's my boobs and ass. Now let me down."

Glaine does so without me having to smack him again.

Once I'm on my feet, though, he braves a fleeting touch, using the edge of his claw to trace the curve of my ass. "It is most voluptuous," he marvels. "I like it."

If he sounded pervy, I'd slap his hand away from me. But since there's an innocence to his tone that makes me think that he means the compliment, I just step away from him.

"Flattering won't work on me," I warn him. "Neither will your ham-handed flirting."

Glaine frowns.

"My hands are made of meat, yes," he says after a moment, and I'm thinking that the translation from English to Sombran is a little wonky there. Just in case, he shows me them. "But my claws are sharp and strong. I don't have my sword, but I can protect you with these."

Those suckers are at least an inch-and-a-half long. I'm actually impressed enough to smile a little as we start heading forward again. Or maybe it's because he's not overruling my autonomy, insisting that he carry me after all. He's letting me walk, and though I'll probably be begging for a piggyback ride by day two of this 'journey', it's not enough of a strike against him for doing what he wants without thinking about what *I* want.

We walk in silence for a little longer before Glaine clears his throat.

I look over at him. "Yes?"

"I think I've understood what it was you said to me before."

"What's that?"

"Flirting."

Okay. "What about it?"

"You mean like how I remind you that I am attracted to you because you're my mate. That is flirting."

My small smile dies. "Something like that."

Up ahead, there's a fire pit. Seriously. That's what Glaine told me it's called. A literal hole in the ash, it's full of fire. I try not to think about what that could mean. Is Sombra all flames, or is it constantly burning? I'm not sure, but he mentions that only the fire-eater demons—a rare subset of Sombra demons—can handle the flame and use that to power the part of this world that doesn't rely on mages and honest-to-God magic. It doesn't really make sense to me, but since I wouldn't run headlong into a fire pit, I just take his warning that we must avoid them and give them a wide berth. Not hard to do when the billowing smoke and renewed rotten egg stink warns you that they're coming.

I wondered if that's all there is to this world when we first left the dungeon and Glaine said it was okay to speak again. That's when he told me that we're heading toward a village made up of Sombra demons, but that while we're leaving the dungeon without Duke Haures's permission—you know, *escaping*—we're purposely keeping to the edge of the shadows because we shouldn't run into anyone else if we do.

I have to rely on him. It sucks, but I have to *trust* him. Do I? If I can believe that he honestly wants to prove that he is my mate, then sure.

But since I just can't accept that Billie Bickles from Manhattan is supposed to be the fated partner to an immortal demon...

Looping the chain around one thick wrist, Glaine moves into me. He's careful not to prick me with his claws as he grabs me by the waist, lifting me up and marching around the next fire pit.

This time, I let him maneuver me without fighting back. It's not the first time he's done this as we fled, and I've learned it's not worth it to argue. He didn't go through all this trouble and piss off his ruler just to lose me now, and I get that.

So I wait until he's decided we're far enough away from the fire pit and sets me down to murmur a 'thanks' before trudging forward in the ash.

He bows his head, drawing attention to his arcing horns. "Of course, Billie."

Damn it. The way he murmurs my name, one part reverential, one part possessive... despite how hot it is out here, I shiver.

Glaine is smart enough not to mention it.

Though he does decide that he's going to attempt to explain his insane rationale to me again. "I think you misunderstand me. I am not attracted to you solely because the gods gave you to me—"

Not this again. At least, with the excuse that we're 'fated mates', it can explain why a seven-foot-tall demon with huge muscles, gleaming horns, pointed ears, and fangs might look at me and think 'sex' and not 'dinner'. Because, oh, yeah... I have no idea how he thinks we could even fit, but there's no doubt in my mind that, when Glaine says 'mate', it's because he's already imagining us fucking.

I'm definitely adventurous, but even I have my limits. I just have to hope that this nice guy act he puts on when he's not glowering down at me in silence is a clue that I really can trust him with *that* when I'm at my most vulnerable. Like sleep. I'm gonna need it sooner or later and—

Pushing those concerns out of my head, I snort.

"You can't tell me that I'm any demon's idea of a mate."

I try not to be so self-deprecating, but after more than fifteen years in Sierra's shadow, it's tough. And I don't blame her one bit for my own insecurities. Like always, I deal.

But it seems as though Glaine won't let me—at least, not alone.

He doesn't need the chains as an excuse to get closer to me. But he takes it, and now he's consuming me. With his gaze, with his masculine scent—spicy and warm and so much nicer than the rotten egg stink —and his possessiveness as he bows his big body over mine.

"You are small. Your ears are rounded." He lays a warm finger on the shell of my ear before I can jerk my head out of his reach. His touch scorches—and I don't just mean my skin, either. "Your fangs are too tiny to do any damage. You are mortal and you can die. I won't allow that, but these are facts. You are a pale shade of red. Your eyes are dim. You are no demoness... but it doesn't matter. Because, to me, you are *perfect*.

"You are perfect because you are Billie. You are also mine." He pats my poor sleep-flattened curls gently, as though I'm a pet... but I get the vibe that, if given the chance, he would've gone for a more intimate touch than on my ear. "Sombra demons *are* immortal. That means we are patient. I have forever to earn your forgiveness and your heart."

He's immortal.

I'm not.

I don't have forever. I don't even have more than the handful of days it's going to take to find a mage to separate us and, hopefully, send me home. Sierra has got to be worried. Roy's probably pulled in his whole security team, searching for me. And Three... I miss my cat. I miss my *phone*. I miss my life.

But when I glance up and see the look on Glaine's face and know—just *know*—that he means what he says... I swallow roughly.

For once, I don't have a pithy comeback.

CHAPTER 9
TRUST ME

BILLIE

don't trust easily. I rarely trust at all. But there are times when I've been thrown into a situation where I have no choice. It's kind of like trauma-bonding in a way, and after a full day of travel... I decide I have to trust Glaine for now otherwise I'll lose it.

I have to trust him to show me the right spot to squat and pee that won't end with fire shooting up my vagina. I have to trust him that the berry-looking things he digs out of the ash are edible; at the very least, they're sweet enough to eat, and juicy enough to quench my thirst. When my legs go wobbly, I have to trust him to pick me up, and when I fall asleep against his chest, I trust him to keep on marching toward Nuit.

He doesn't need the sleep, he assures me. We don't need to hunker down because both of us must rest. He'll sleep when we reach the mage's village. Until then, he will do what he promised and get me there.

We're not as alone out here in the shadows as I first thought. The way I see it, the sooner we're in a village, the better, and if he wants to keep on trucking... well, I'm not going to stop him.

Not even when it becomes obvious that we're being followed...

"What was that?"

I know what I just saw. I've been noticing creatures like that skittering by us earlier, with the same white eyes, only they're a lot smaller. He told me about the prey beasts that lurk closer to the edge of the shadows where we are because, if they venture too much deeper into the blackness that surrounds us, there are even more dangerous monsters to deal with.

The arkoda is one. The hitchul is another. The ungez are the smaller ones that scamper like squirrels, and when I heard a long, drawn-out squawk that broke up the heavy silence at one point, he simply said, "Firebird."

That's not a bird tracking us. The shadowy figure has horns and two long arms. It's a similar size and shape to Glaine, and it reminds me of the shadow form that Sombra demons at the palace wore.

Its shoulders are hunched a little, almost as though

it's preparing itself to fall forward on all fours and run if it has to, but based on the few times I've caught its silhouette and those eyes staring at us... it—*he* can match our pace easily.

And he's following us.

The second I spoke, the creature pauses. Then he growls. Stepping out of the shadows in the distance, the glow from the reddish moon above us illuminates him.

It's a demon alright. And though most of his features melt together in his shadows, I can make out details. His hands are flexed, shadowy claws on display. His nose is shorter than Glaine's, his hair longer, and because he *is* in his shadows, he's not covering anything up.

How do I know? Because unless he's got a baseball bat or something swinging between his legs, that's his cock.

I yip, and as I watch, that part of his shadowy anatomy jolts and starts to lift.

Fuck. He sees me and that's how his body reacts? What is it with these demons? Do they all have a human fetish, or is it just because I'm the only female I've seen in Sombra so far?

I don't know, but I start to retreat.

Glaine holds out his hand. "Billie. Don't move."

Okay. There are times when I'll cross my arms over my chest and refuse to be ordered around. There are times when I'll pretend not to hear a command so that I'm not necessarily disobeying. And there are times when I know when to keep my mouth shut and do what I'm told.

In the shadows of Sombra, with the creepy white-eyed demon moving like he's some kind of *beast* as he stalks us as his prey... this is one of those times.

Don't move? I'll try. I mean, the length of chain separating me and Glaine is about as much distance as I can keep from him. If he moves, I'll have to follow—

The white-eyed demon takes a deep breath in. His exhale is a sudden roar that has my knees turning to jelly. I wobble, about to drop because my other instinct is to turn and run as far as I can in the opposite direction, and that's when Glaine—grumpy, scowling, silent Glaine when he's not attempting to 'flirt' with me—throws his head back, shakes it roughly, and howls with more emotion than I've seen him give off since I first rejected him.

Something happens. The big, red-skinned demon seems to grow impossibly bigger before he explodes; at least, that's what it seems like from my vantage point behind his big, bulky back. The golden chains gleam, the glow so bright I squint against it, and when I recover my sight, Glaine is gone.

No. Not gone. He's reverted to that mass of shadows, the silhouette of the horned demon who walked out of my kitchen before he abducted me.

I don't know what shocks me more: that after almost three days stuck together, he's broken out of the chains—or that, once he's free, the first thing he does is charge toward the demon who's been stalking us.

They're shadows. It doesn't matter that he was able to grab my arm when he pulled me into the portal that brought me here. When Glaine is red-skinned with the ridges over his nose and on his brow, I can think of him as at least human*ish*. As a mass of black shadows with a pair of glowing green stoplights for eyes? My mind just can't comprehend that he's anything but a grumpy storm cloud.

I expect them to meet and become one big shadow. Not even close. They collide, the ground shaking with the force of their strike. Their shoulders slam into each other first, using brute force to knock down their opponent. When that doesn't work, they lower their heads and ram their horns into each other repeatedly while snarling at each other in Sombran—and what might not be Sombran but pure animalistic sounds.

It goes on like that for a few fierce moments before Glaine scores a hit. Something cracks, a piece of horn goes flying, and the howl of rage from the white-eyed demon is deafening.

Glaine retreats for a moment, then glances around. His eyes land on me, and he bobs his in-tact horns. He's making sure I'm safe, but just as I want to shout at him not to be distracted, he waves his hand. It darkens with even more shadows, and when they clear, he's holding a gleaming silver sword about two feet long.

What the— where did *that* come from?

I don't know, but I'm glad to see it. The two demons seemed evenly matched when they were ramming horns with each other, but now my demon soldier has the edge—

Seeing the sword, the other demon gnashes his fangs and, slashing out with his claws, goes for Glaine's wrist.

The sword falls to the ash.

Damn it!

He was distracted after all, wasn't he? All because he was looking for me.

Barely taking his eyes off of the challenger for a moment, Glaine searches for me for a second time, and, just as the demon tackles him *hard*, he rears back his foot and punts the hilt of the sword, sending it flying in my direction.

Glaine is on his back, the rogue demon snarling in Sombran on top of him, digging his claws into Glaine's shadows.

The big demon howls, throwing the other one off, but the white-eyed demon launches himself at Glaine right away.

"Stab him," bellows Glaine—in English. "He will take you for his own if he guts me first."

I drop down, grabbing the sword from the ash.

Glaine grabs the rogue demon's remaining horn, twisting his head so that he has the leverage to rise up. I don't know if he's been hurt or not. Can a shadow be hurt? This sword suggests that it can.

And Glaine wants me to stab this other demon?

I... I don't know. Can I?

I hesitate, and the rogue demon senses weakness. Twisting out of Glaine's hold, he butts the soldier in the middle with his horn, then plants his foot in his side, kicking my demon at least ten feet through the air.

Glaine lands on the ash with a thump and a roar, but the rogue demon is already on the move. He spins on his heel once Glaine is down again, tearing through the ash right toward me.

"Billie!"

I tighten my grip on the sword.

I can't let this demon get me. I also can't let him hurt Glaine anymore. He's immortal, so he shouldn't be able to die, but the duke mentioned that he could easily end his existence if he chose to. With a sword like this? Or being gored to death by a pair of claws?

No. I can't let anything like that happen. Glaine... he's my ticket out of here. His only mistake was getting it in his head that *I* was his mate after he went searching for that spell book he was talking about. And, okay. He wants me to believe that he followed the book to our apartment because *Sierra* has a mate of her own. It's not Glaine, though.

And if the pit of my stomach did a little flip-flop in inexplicable relief to hear that, for once, someone would rather be with me than Sierra? I'm sure I haven't noticed at all...

The demon has slowed, circling me now. Taunting me. He sees the sword and doesn't give a shit. Because he doesn't think I'll use it? Or because he's just toying with both of us?

My arms shake, but I don't drop the sword.

"Don't hesitate if given the chance," commands Glaine. "He is lost. Better my sword end his existence than the fate Duke Haures would have in store for him."

In answer, the demon spits something at me in Sombran, then jerks on what has to be his dick to make sure I get the message despite having no idea what he's saying.

That does it.

I hold up the sword, and Glaine calls out, "You can do this, Billie. I trust you."

He does?

I firm my grip on the hilt. "Bring it," I dare the rogue.

He has no idea what I'm saying. It doesn't matter. His eyes glow so brightly, they light up his face. It's misshapen. I suddenly understand what the word 'demonic' means. His fangs are overgrown, his cheeks stretched tight, and there is a promise in his blank gaze that he will hurt me—and he will enjoy it.

No.

At the same time as a burst of adrenaline has me dashing forward, the rogue demon runs full speed at me. I don't even have to move the sword or do anything but angle it up before it's slicing right through the shadows, getting lodged in the meat of the solid chest beneath.

He gasps, and I can't help but wonder if this was some sort of demon suicide before I realize that I'm still holding the sword and he's skewered on it like a shish kebob.

I yell and drop the sword. For a second, he's still standing. In the next? He crumples to the ash.

I dash away. Without the chains, I could keep running, but I stop when I've put a good distance between me and the rogue demon. Glaine, meanwhile, has gotten up. Limping for a few steps before shaking it off and striding the rest of the way toward the fallen demon, he crouches down at his side. He murmurs something in Sombran, then, with a yank, pulls his sword out.

He does something else to the demon with the blade. A little late to be squeamish, but I cover my eyes with my fingers for a moment. He grunts, and when he's done, he's hovering there in his shadows while that other demon is... gone.

No. He's not gone. Unless I'm imagining it, there's a massive mound of ash lying in just the right size and shape as the fallen demon. As I watch, it disintegrates further and joins the piles of ash beneath it.

My head shoots up to Glaine. He's brushing his hands together as he moves away from the ash.

"There," he says. "I've returned my sword to my shadows until we have need of it again."

Holy crap. I don't know what he did or where he pulled that sword from, but if it's an immortal demon *killer,* we should keep it out. Not because I have any intention to use it on Glaine next—I'm pissed at him, sure, but that was pure self-defense that had me stabbing the demon, not a desire for revenge—but because I like the idea of being able to protect myself without relying on him.

"What? No. I think—"

It doesn't matter what I think because, before I can say another word, something *else* happens.

CHAPTER 10
ESSENCE EXCHANGE

BILLIE

Glaine shudders and, suddenly, he's gone from being a good twenty feet away from me to *right there*.

The chains heat up enough to be noticeable, though it barely stings as the metal goes from dark gold to vivid red, then to the constant gold glimmer I've gotten used to.

Just like the big demon attached to the other end of it, a thick manacle around his just as thick wrist, is the Glaine from before.

He reaches up into his hairline, fingers landing lightly on the nearest horn.

"You didn't lose a horn," I blurt out, as though

guessing why he reached up the moment he was solid again. "It was his."

Glaine drops his hand. "Another reason it was a mercy to send him back to the shadows."

My frown makes it obvious that I don't understand, but instead of reminding me that I wouldn't be as lost if I let him give me his essence, he answers my unasked question.

"He was fully demonic so he might not have noticed, but a challenge that ends with a broken horn makes it clear which demon lost the battle. It would've taken centuries for his to grow back, and if he survived as long, it would've been with the stigma of a male who was too weak to protect that which he cared for."

Like a mate, I bet.

I wait for Glaine to point out the obvious. That he still has both his horns, the other demon is ash, and I don't have a single scratch on me—and all because of that weapon. When he doesn't, I do.

"What the hell was that sword?"

"A gift from Duke Haures to his favored guard. Thankfully, he didn't think to ask for its return before he put us both in the dungeon. I kept it for safe-keeping in my shadows, but once the chains were gone, I grabbed it."

Yeah. Thankfully.

And about those chains...

"Did you know you could escape from them?" To

me, that's more important than the stupid sword. "Can you take the chains off anytime you want?"

Can you take them off *now*?

So maybe I'm stuck with this manacle on my wrist until we can find a mage we can convince to take it off. But if Glaine can go shadowy after all and slip out of it like he did, he might as well. Why stay chained to me if he doesn't have to?

And, okay. I know the answer to *that* one. He's convinced I'm his mate. As long as I'm stuck to him like this, he has the chance to find a way to get me to agree. Not likely, but it's a lot easier to use Stockholm syndrome to his advantage when he tries to save me by coming between me and another demon, then trusts me enough to stab the rogue instead of taking the chance to plunge the sword in his back instead.

I would never. I don't hate Glaine. This is just a shitty circumstance. He lives in a world where he's spent centuries—*centuries*—believing that, if he did his duty, his gods would reward him with one female to be his forever mate. He believes that's me, and according to his traditions and his customs, he's just acting like any other demon male would.

It's me that's not acting the way I'm supposed to— at least, to Glaine, I'm not. I get the idea that, in this world, when a demon recognizes his fated mate, it's expected that she does the same. And if you know that you're looking at the one guy meant for you, what's the point in waiting? That I haven't already tried to sleep with him just makes Glaine think that he's done something wrong, and that nothing will stop him from fixing it.

He's trying. I'll give him that. He's trying, and with the little he knows about me from my essence, it's working.

Damn it.

All I've wanted was someone to pick me. To *see* me. To choose me.

And, fuck it, to trust me.

With that heavy sword in my hand, he told me he trusted me. And how did I react? I stabbed a demon for him.

How much do you want to bet that, to a male like Glaine, that's like saying 'I love you'?

But if he's been lying to me...

"I fed enough of my essence to the charmed chain to escape it long enough to protect you, my wee mortal. Worry not. I shouldn't suffer the same effects as the hunter."

I have no idea what he's talking about—or what that has to do with anything. "Hunter? What hunter?"

Glaine's eyes dim slightly. "See? This is why you need my essence. With it, you would know."

"Or you could just tell me instead of making everything so damn difficult," I snap.

Sue me. I just stabbed a demon, then watched

Glaine finish him off. And while I could pretend he was no better than an animal or some kind of monster human who attacks women from the shadows, I'm still shaky and in no mood to play these games.

Glaine can tell.

"I'm sorry, Billie," he rumbles, and look at that: he's not allergic after all. "His name is Nox. A hunter from Nuit. He was put in the dungeon for many human years, but when he sensed his mate in need of him, he fed nearly all of his essence to the chains to escape them. More than he should've. Now, he no longer can control his forms. Solid... shadow... he's lost that power, but gained a mate." He sets his jaw. "It was worth it for him. If that's what happens to me, it will also be worth it."

Oh. Okay, then.

"What if you give more to the chain?" I ask. "Will that break it?"

"For a time. I told you, Billie, and I didn't lie: there are two ways to break the chain."

Right. A mage has to remove it—or I have to accept that I am his mate. He bonds his soul to mine, making it so that the first law of Sombra doesn't apply to us, and the chains will vanish.

Those chains will, but I'll have a demon-sized shadow that I'll never be able to get rid of.

Literally.

"No matter how much essence I feed it, they

will return. But I can never give it all of my essence because, no matter how long it takes, I will save a drop for you. I will cling to the hope that you will see me as a male worthy of you. That you will take my essence, take my cock, take my seed... take everything I am and accept me as your male."

My stomach tightens, and no, those aren't butterflies flapping at the earnest yet determined way he admits that he's waiting for the day he gets to fuck me. Too bad that sex with a demon comes with a little side effect: that permanent second shadow.

I do my best to ignore that last part. Instead, I focus on what he's also saying—that the chains being gone is temporary unless I bond him to me. Now, I'm not doing that. I'm still holding out hope that that mage we're heading to can give us a twofer: taking off the chain and sending me back home.

But I'm still curious about his essence.

"How much do you have now?"

"Enough that, if you accept it, you'll understand Sombran as if it is your tongue. You'll know the dangers of my realm without my having to explain them to you."

Oh, Glaine... you're a wily demon, aren't you?

"Won't the chain stop you from giving it to me?" I get the impression that it's more to punish the weak mortal and that's why we're wearing it, but that the charm in the chains does keep him from accessing his demon magic.

"That's the one thing it can't do. The magic is tied to our essences, but a Sombra demon's instincts are more powerful than even that. You are my mate, Billie. My body cries out to share my essence with you. Not even the golden chains will be able to keep it from going where it belongs."

I glance down. Can't help it. Thankfully, the chains don't stop him from covering his lower half in tightly woven shadowy leather-looking pants, either. Because when he says his body is crying out to give me his essence... that's not all he wants to give me, I'm betting.

Sex is out. My relationship with my demon kidnapper is already way too complicated for me to satisfy my curiosity when it comes to what he's packing beneath those shadows. Is he proportionate in size and a monster down there, too? Does he have one cock? Two? Something that buzzes? I'd be lying if I said my imagination hasn't already run wild when it comes to that, but I quickly stopped that line of thought before Glaine guesses and decides to be helpful and *show* me. Now I've seen the outline of that rogue demon and can answer at least *one* of those questions...

Essence, Billie. His soul. He already took yours, and he's offering you his.

Damn it. He's not wrong. I don't know what I'm doing, and while I've trusted him as much as I can, if I have all of his knowledge about this world, I can be a lot more independent.

Okay.

Let's do it.

I hold out my hand before I lose the nerve.

Glaine hesitates for a moment, then takes my hand in his huge one. It heats up, then I suck in a breath when a massive electrical shock jolts me.

I yank my hand back as everything he is slams right into me. I stumble, but I stay standing even without his steadying touch on my elbow.

He waits a few moments before asking me, "How do you feel?"

I wish he didn't sound so concerned. Where's that forceful, commanding demon who did what he wanted and didn't care about the repercussions for anyone else? And, true, I got that impression of him after he stole me, but before we could communicate. Suddenly, I know that while the demon soldier *is* used to being in command, he grabbed me more out of a panic that he would lose me before he ever had the chance to confess that we were meant to be mates.

And how do I know? Because he's just stuffed my head full of his memories and his emotions, the very essence of who Glaine is.

How do I feel? Like I'm hungover. My head is heavy. I don't like the sensation of not knowing which thought is mine. I'm so used to being the only one in my head and, after a moment to settle, I use every bit of mental strength I have to shove Glaine's essence to the far back of my mind.

I'm panting by the time I'm done. It's tough. Harder than killing that demon out of self-defense, and isn't that something I'm going to unpack when I'm back home and can call my therapist... but I do it, and tapping into my Thr33peat days, I give Glaine a smile that once graced the covers of hundreds of teeny-bopper mags.

"Feel great," I lie, not even caring that he can probably use my essence to tell that I am. "Why?"

GLAINE

I want to believe I am an honorable male.

An honorable male would have warned his mate that, unless the bond is finalized and the mate promise given shortly after an essence exchange, we shall feel unfulfilled. It's the gods' way of reminding a Sombra demon that a mate is a precious gift, and must not be wasted. To spark a bond but not finish it... it is as though we are throwing that gift in the face of the gods, mocking them. A demon must be fully bonded to his mate after the exchange or he must release his female, otherwise we will suffer until we do.

It's the mate sickness, and it's not very common among demons and demonesses. When a demon finds his mate in a demoness, she has been raised to understand that her essence must be guarded until she is ready to finalize a bond. The same with the demon. But humans... I want to believe I am an honorable male, but while I had Billie's essence first, she did not know exactly what she was agreeing to when she took mine.

Oh, I was careful. I let her know that, once the exchange was done, she wouldn't be able to continue denying that I am her mate. My stubborn female understood, but I knew she didn't quite believe me. She doubted that any consequences she might face wouldn't be worth it for her to have an equal footing in my world.

If I could keep her from suffering the mate sickness, I would. And maybe I *am* honorable, because I mean that. The seconds when I thought Billie was in danger of the rogue demon... I hated myself for leaving her vulnerable. She didn't know what he said to her in Sombran, or how he promised to take her as his own mate, taking his own pleasure as often and as roughly as he wanted before he tossed the broken mortal to the shadows.

He deserved the fate he met with my sword. To even threaten Billie... to think that she was as much a dumb beast as those that lurk in the shadows because she is human... to say he would take his pleasure from her and not worship her the way I will?

He deserved his fate, just as Billie deserved to be the one to give it to him.

But I have been arrogant. I've decided to take my mate instead of waiting for her to find me. Her presence in Sombra is an insult to Duke Haures and our gods… and they've both punished me for it.

Worse, they've punished my mate.

Mere hours after I gave her my essence, she starts to slow. It is hot in Sombra for my mortal, but her curls have drooped, drenched in sweat. The air smells of salt, and also her own delectable musk as she becomes more and more aroused… and I have to breathe softly so that I don't show her how the mate sickness is also affecting me.

Finally, just when I was prepared to suggest we find a closed ring of shadows where we can sit for a moment and rest, she stops.

Because she does, I do.

Billie exhales. "I'm sorry. I know I'm dragging, and I don't want you to have to carry me while I can walk… but, crap. I'm not feeling the best right now."

From what I've learned about Billie, through her essence and from being so close to her these last few days, it is a miracle that she admitted as much to me. But I've been watching her closely since I gave her my essence, and though I hoped the chains would dull the mate sickness, or there would be more time before it struck… I know that I must tell her the truth.

"It is the mate sickness," I admit.

"I knew this wasn't normal." She narrows her eyes at me. "What did you do to me?"

"It wasn't me. It's the gods—"

Billie pushes her damp curls out of her voice so that she can glare even harder. "The gods want me to get laid?" At my blank look, she elaborates. "Sex. They want us to fuck. Is that what you're trying to tell me?"

Fuck?

Mate.

Ah. So she does understand. "Yes. They've matched us together as mates. They've given us a bond to grow and nurture. But we've neglected it. Now that the essence exchange is complete, they're reminding us how we will fulfill the bond."

"So what? You gave me your essence to make me horny as hell?"

I glance at the top of her curls. "You don't have any horns," I say gently. "I don't mind. You are attractive to me without them. But though I can make you immortal with our bond, I cannot give you horns."

Billie stamps her foot in frustration, then hisses in a breath when her breasts jiggle. She cups them, then scowls when she sees that my attention has dropped there. "I know I don't have horns, Glaine. That's not what I meant. You did something to me and now I feel like, if I don't have sex, I'm gonna hurl. That is not okay."

I... I know. "We don't have to mate. That will ease the mate sickness, but it's not the only way to calm it."

Her expression turns to one of surprise. "Wow. I would've thought you'd go straight to your dick being magic enough that it's the only cure. Okay. I'll bite. What else can I do to get rid of this?"

"A touch should help."

Billie shoves her free hand toward me.

I clear my throat. "An intimate touch is best."

Her delicate little face hardens. "I knew it. Let me guess. You shoving your dick in me is the intimate touch you have in mind? Or will you take your time with me first, using a finger or two to stretch me out?"

I hate hearing the venom in her face, especially since I've caused it. "I know you are small. We will fit. I know of other demons with human mates who have no problem pleasuring each other. But I will not claim you until you ask me to—"

She huffs. "How nice of you."

I continue imploringly, hoping to convince my mate that she can trust me as I trust her. "We don't need to mate. Any intimate touch will do... but, if you'll allow it, I can use my mouth."

Billie's ridge-free forehead wrinkles. "Your mouth?" she says suspiciously. "Where?"

"On your cunt. I know, that must seem strange to a mortal, but I assure you... it is done in Sombra. A male is born to pleasure his female with his mouth."

"Oh. I *know*. That's not why I'm shocked, Glaine. I just... wow. I was with Trevor for a year and he never offered to go down on me."

"Let's not talk of Trevor," I rumble. "You are my mate. If you allow it, I will show you exactly why a Sombra demon is better for you than some worthless mortal who was foolish enough to lose you."

I'm bluffing. I have never pleasured a female with my mouth before, and if she searches my essence, she will see that. Still, it's instinctive. Once a male gets his female's taste... he knows what to do.

"Okay, fine. It's not worth talking about that tool anyway. But you... did you mean it? You like to eat pussy?"

An image of a creature not unlike an ungez flashes through my mind, quickly replaced by that of the juncture between Billie's legs. Her slinky coverings have shifted once or twice, giving me a peek that I quickly looked away from, but I imagine it is not so very different than the drawings passed around the barracks to young demon males.

"Are you asking me if I would like to taste your cunt?" I dart out my tongue, licking my bottom lip. "I will be honest with you, my Billie. Because it is your cunt, I will say that I would love it. But... I have never done it before. I've never *mated* before."

I couldn't because I hadn't yet found my one true mate.

Her eyes widen. "Wow. Okay. Wasn't expecting that. But, hey, don't worry." Reaching down, shimmying her dress up so that I can see her cunt for the first time as the perfume from her arousal fills my nostrils, she smiles encouragingly at me. "I'll show you what I like."

I go still. "Is that a yes?"

"If it's going to get rid of this sickness, Glaine, it's a hell yes."

That is all I need to hear.

I won't lay Billie down on the ash. Without access to my shadows, I can't conceal her in them or wrap her up in them. There is no one near so I'm not worried about others watching as I pleasure her. However, she doesn't like being covered in the ash anymore than she has to, so I decide instead to grab her by her waist and lift her high.

With one command—"Take hold of my horns"—I settle her so that her legs are over my shoulders, and her cunt is right in front of my nose.

She has hair there. Curls the same shade as those on her head, though they're not as soft, I notice, when I bury my nose past them, searching for the source of her musk, and groaning when I find that she is cool and slick and waiting for me.

Females produce a cream to let their males know that they are ready to be taken. I cannot mate Billie now, but I use my tongue to gather up as much as I can.

I growl against her skin. She is *delicious*.

Tugging my horns, Billie lets out a sound that is half-squeal, half-laugh. It is a mortal sound of delight, and when I dip the point of my tongue into the true source of her musk... when I find the entrance to her cunt and attempt to mimic what I would do with my cock if she gave me the opportunity... she squeezes her legs around my head while panting, "Yes. Don't stop, don't *stop*."

As you wish, Billie.

I would lick her, taste her, suck her for all eternity if I could. But, sooner than I hope, she writhes against me, squeezing my horns as her pants become soft little mews before she shudders and finally relaxes against me.

A few moments later, Billie taps me on the horn. "Okay," she says, her voice breathless. "I'm good. You can put me down now."

I don't want to. She has found her release and, in it, also relief from the mate sickness. That means I must release her even knowing that, if I could spend the rest of my days with my face between my mate's thighs, I would. I hunger for her taste... but, more than that, I want to show her that I can be an honorable male.

So instead of licking her cunt again, I nuzzle her curls, then set her back on her feet.

Billie wobbles. I catch her, and preen when she doesn't shove me away.

"Are you well, my mate?"

She nods absently, and I'm even prouder that I licked much of her sharp tongue out of her. If that's all it takes to tame my feisty mortal... I look forward to giving her as much pleasure with my mouth as she will allow.

But then, lifting her hand, gesturing at something behind me, I discover that it is not because of me and my prowess that she is so distracted.

"Hey, Glaine. I thought we had another day to go to get to Nuit."

"Yes."

"And we're not near any other villages, right?"

I purposely led Billie away from other demons in case they warned Duke Haures we had been past. "We are not."

"That's what I thought. So, uh, what's that?"

I follow her point, and my heart sinks.

In all my existence, I've only ever come across that den once before. It was during a routine patrol through the shadows, and a young, inexperienced Glaine knocked to make sure its inhabitants were in no need of one of Duke Haures's guards.

It was also the first time I came face to face with a pair of demon twins—and the last.

Until now.

BILLIE

"The doppelseers," he breathes out.

Dopp-ul-see-ers? It must be a Sombra word without a direct translation in English because, when Glaine just about whispers it, there's a harsh edge to each of the four syllables that marks it as another foreign one. Like when a fluent speaker of a second language just slips a word of their own into a conversation because it's easier than trying to explain it in mine.

Context clues, Billie. Come on. You travel all over the world and have to broker contracts and meetings in dozens of languages. Sure, I have Charlotte's help, but Sierra's lawyer is back in New York. I have to parse these situations out on my own.

Doppel... Double, maybe? If a doppelgänger is like a twin, what can a doppelseer be? Someone who sees double?

Maybe. Let's go with that.

I don't know how I didn't see their house before. It melds into the shadows, no windows reflecting the moonlight, and with only a single door. Built like an old-fashioned cabin, it's squat and wide, but the moment I glanced in that direction, it was there like it has always been.

But I know it wasn't. Before Glaine knocked me momentarily senseless with that fantastic tongue of his, I was looking around, keeping an eye out for any other rogue demons who might catch on to the fact that I was so aroused, I could just about hear my thighs squeak while we were walking.

It was bad. Like, taking an aphrodisiac bad. If Glaine had solemnly told me that the only way to stop the empty ache in my pussy, plus the fever and the sweats, was to sleep with him, I might've actually gone ahead and bent over for the growly demon. My body was telling me that's what it needed, this strange feeling in my chest was tugging me toward Glaine, and my pussy was screaming, "Go, Billie, go."

I got what I needed by clinging to his horns for dear life as I rode his face. It's probably going to be a lot harder to convince him that I'm not his mate after that which is why I was actually a little relieved to have a distraction once he set me back down on my feet.

Then I catch a glimpse of Glaine's strained expression out of the corner of my eye, add that to the sudden inexplicable appearance of a cabin I *know* wasn't there before, and I'm beginning to think this might not be the sort of distraction I had in mind.

Glaine is seven feet tall, can wield a sword when the chains aren't dulling his shadow magic, and is strong as hell. He's also a trained soldier who didn't blink at ordering me to stab the rogue. If he's alarmed by this cabin, what the hell's inside?

Doppelseers. Okay. Sure.

Keeping my voice low, just in case, I murmur, "What are the doppelseers?"

"The doppelseers are the voice of the gods here on Sombra."

So they're a 'who'. I think I understand. "Like priests?"

Glaine mulls it over for a moment. "Priests serve the gods in your world. The gods need none of that in Sombra so Lucian and Damien serve the duke like the rest of us."

Why am I not surprised to hear that? "Okay. So we have to worry about them turning us in?"

"Not necessarily."

I glance back at the cabin. "Do we have to worry

about the fact that their cabin seems to have just popped up out of nowhere?"

When he doesn't deny that, I know we're in trouble.

And then he says, "Duke Haures is a bondmaster. He has very unique magic."

I nod. Okay. If he says so.

"But the doppelseers have magic unlike any other demons in our realm, including Duke Haures. His palace stays put in Mavro. Lucian and Damien... they go wherever they're needed."

I... don't think I like the way he said that.

"Do *we* need them?"

Glaine takes a deep breath. "They are diviners. Many clans have seers, but the doppelseers are the most respected visionaries in Sombra." He lowers his voice even deeper, sounding almost reverential as he does. "They're supposed to be the longest-living demons left on Sombra, older than even Duke Haures."

Supposed to be... "You don't know for sure?"

"No one knows except the doppelseers."

I'll admit, this is actually really interesting to me. Not only because Glaine seems so cock-sure about everything that it's new for him to admit there's something he *doesn't* know, but because I'm looking at the most ancient of demon immortals who have their own traveling house.

I loved *Howl's Moving Castle* as a kid. Is this like that?

"Do we get to meet them?" I ask.

Glaine sighs. "They appeared to us. Trust me. That is an invitation we would be foolish to refuse."

As if the doppelseers have been able to listen in on our conversation, the door to the cabin creaks open.

Glaine sets his shoulders. "Come, Billie. And whatever you do? Don't ask about their eyes."

THAT'S NOT THE ONLY WHISPERED WARNING GLAINE gives me as we trudge over to the open cabin door, but it's the one I'm repeating in my head as I'm led into a cozy interior awash with orange light.

Like at the palace, the doppelseers have floating orbs that illuminate their space. And, like at the palace, they're in their shadow forms as so many of the other demons I've met have been. That doesn't make it any less obvious that they're identical twins... well, *almost* identical.

One demon has a bright white eye for the left one and a glowing purple one for the right. His brother? Has the opposite.

It's freaky. Sorry. Maybe it's my experience with the rogue and how Glaine explained you can tell when a Sombra demon has gone fully demonic by the whites of his eyes. In Sombra, their eyes are like mood rings, only they tell you what kind of demon you're dealing with. Only the duke has blue eyes, while mages are purple, soldiers are green, and hunters are red.

And seers... they have *that*.

"Glaine." That's the demon with the right eye that's purple. "It's good to see you in the flesh again after all these centuries."

Huh? Okay. That explains how he recognized the cabin. Could also explain why he's on his guard around the demon twins. I can't wait to ask him about it. Something tells me there's definitely history here.

It's especially obvious in the respectful way he bows his head. "Lucian."

Lucian's twin nods a greeting. He has the left eye that's purple, and to make it worse, I don't think he ever blinks.

Glaine addresses him next. "Damien. Anything for me?"

Damien shakes his head. I guess that's a no.

Glaine almost looks relieved to hear it—and that's when Lucian gestures toward the stairs behind him.

Wait. What?

There were no stairs. One hundred percent, they were not there two seconds ago. More magic, huh?

"We have seen that the demon guard and his mortal mate are in need of shadows since they don't have any of their own. You are safe with us. The duke will not be able to see you until we allow him to."

Glaine looks surprised. "You're concealing us?"

Lucian's purple eye flares. *Only* the purple one. "We have been. We will be. There is something... we have seen your mortal before. She is known to us."

I am? Oh, great. Demon soothsayers. I can only imagine what they've seen.

Glaine kicks his chin up. "You have seen that she is my mate."

Damien shakes his head again.

"My twin is right," says Lucian. "When it comes to your prophecy, I do not think anything has changed. But we will see. Come. Rest. You will spend two full moons as our guest. When they are done, journey on to Nuit. That should be all the time we need to read the female."

Yeah. I'm not so sure I like the sound of that. Glaine might have warned me to pretend their eyes aren't freaky, but he also said not to draw their attention to me if I can help it. Read me... I don't know what they'll see, but I'd rather they kept those purple peepers to themselves.

"Um. Read me?"

"Yes. When I look at you," Lucian says, his voice as deep a rumble as Glaine's, "I see red."

I blink. "Red? Like Glaine?" I gesture behind me.

"Sombra's sky? That's red." A terrible thought pops in my head. "Blood? Is it blood?"

"I do not know," admits Lucian. "I see red. I need to know more. You will stay with us and surround the cabin with your essence." His gaze darts over to Glaine. "You have the mortal's. You will stay, too."

Not like he has a choice. With the chains still keeping us tethered, Glaine's not going anywhere that I'm not... unless they can--

Lucian shakes his head. He has straight black hair even longer than Glaine's, reaching the small of his muscular back. It sways as he moves before seeming to get lost in the edge of his shadowy form. "Our powers are vast, but the chains are not our domain. Apologies, mortal."

Oh, great. Not only can they 'read' people and see the future, but it seems like they can read minds.

I sneak a peek over at the other demon. Since we've been in their front room, he's focused on me. *Only* me. I think he's blinked three times since I've been paying attention. His purple eye seems to be flashing, but apart from when he nodded at Glaine, all of his attention has been sent my way. He still hasn't said a single word, either.

Until I meet his gaze. I can't help but wonder what it is he's picking up on me. It never really dawned on me that, with my essence, I don't have any secrets with Glaine; at least, none of my own. He technically knows everything about me, but he's been careful not to remind me of that.

When Damien tilts his head slightly, cocking his horns in my direction, I get the idea that he knows things about me that even *I* don't know.

And then, in a voice that's surprisingly soft and lyrical, he says, "Out of the spotlight, it's time you rely on a heart barely used."

My mouth falls open even as the demon at my side grows puzzled.

I'm not.

Glaine warned me. One twin spoke in riddles when he spoke at all, the other made it as clear as he possibly could when giving his visions. I'd say it was easy to figure out who was who, but that wasn't a riddle.

That's an altered line from Whiskey Rose's most famous song, 'Heart Barely Used'.

The real one is: *in the spotlight, I'll shine with a heart barely used*, but it's close enough that I can't *not* recognize it. Is it a prophecy? His way of letting me know that he's in my head, too? A reminder for me what's at stake?

"I--"

Lucian smiles at me, cutting me off. "Do not give up hope, wee mortal. For now, rest. We have food and shelter for our guests, and if you take the stairs, the bathwater is running. The tub is waiting for you."

Do I know what the demon riddler means? No.

Would I rather channel Charlotte and start interrogating the doppselseers? Definitely. But if I needed further proof that they're already reading me, I get it in Lucian's sly statement.

The bathwater is running and the tub is waiting? All right. He's got me. I'm covered in ash, I stink like sweat, and this dress has been plastered to my skin for days.

I point in front of me. "Those stairs right there?"

Lucian nods.

I shake my wrist. "Come on, Glaine. Let's go."

***

THE STAIRS LEAD TO A SECOND FLOOR THAT, AFTER THE last couple of days, is Sombra's version of five-star accommodations. A wooden table with a pair of stools is set to the side. There are three different platters of what must be food; I recognize the berries we've been snacking on in the shadows, cooked meat similar to what I choked down in the dungeon, and a plate of greens that could pass for a Sombra salad. Two carafes of liquids—one clear, one purple—are in the center, with two drinking glasses.

On the other side, there is a piece of furniture that I can only describe as a giant bean bag chair. It's round and lumpy, with a furry covering. It looks soft, though, and big enough that both Glaine and I can nestle in the center of it and not touch.

I already know that we'll have to both lay on it together because of the chains. Whether Glaine will sleep or not is a different matter. As far as I can tell, he hasn't since we met, though he scoffed when I asked, telling me that soldiers specifically are trained to go three or four moons without rest before they need it.

It was one thing when he was able to hoist me up in his arms and carry me while we were escaping toward Nuit. I'm only human. If a woman could run on spite, caffeine, and a super busy schedule instead of sleep, Billie Bickles would've given up the five hours I allow myself to get every night a long time ago. There's always something to do, and I only rest because exhaustion is no joke. I know. I've been hospitalized for it twice, and only Sierra threatening to add on to her management team if I didn't take better care of myself managed to get me to realize that there are simply twenty-four hours in a day, and I can't expect to work for twenty-three of them.

Can you blame me? I didn't trust anyone to keep her best interests at heart. After her mother stole all of her royalties and proceeds from her time in Thr33peat, and her previous manager turned out to be just as scummy, I made sure I got my MB because I have *always* looked out for Sierra.

She needed me to slow down. I did. I *tried*. But all

that to say that I do know my own limits... now. I need sleep, and if that meant I had to trust the demon who stole me to keep me safe while I was vulnerable, I did that, too.

That's one plus to him believing I'm meant to be his mate. If there's one thing I can trust him to do, it's watch over me.

And as I squeal before turning to check out the steaming water in a demon-sized bathtub made out of thick crystal tucked against the corner closest to the 'bed', it dawns on me that—if I want to dunk inside of the oversized tub and scrub all the ash off of me—I have to do that with Glaine right there.

My stomach jumps. Worse, it flutters a little.

We didn't get the chance to discuss the mate sickness in depth. I want to. I need to know exactly what Glaine did to me, and what I can expect. Earlier, I was too amped up to care. All I wanted was relief, and if that came in the form of a towering demon with a wicked tongue and the ability to obliterate my pussy without slicing me open with his fangs, fine. I was feverish. Every nerve in my body was twanging. I *ached*, and though an orgasm seemed a little too convenient a cure, I'd be lying if I said I wasn't glad to have the excuse to let him touch me.

There. I'll admit it. While Glaine's demon appearance definitely caught me off-guard at first, there's something about him that keeps luring me closer, like a moth being drawn to a flame. I know I'll be burned. I don't even know if it's me that's feeling something for him or this 'mate bond' that I'm beginning to question.

Throw in the mate sickness and there's no doubt that his mouth on me knocked my discomfort and my nausea aside. In fact, I felt *fantastic*, and if it wasn't for noticing the cabin in the distance, I'm not sure I wouldn't have gone back for seconds.

Now I have my chance and I... no. It was amazing, but it was a mistake. It had to be. If it happens again, I'll grab Glaine's thick finger in my grip. He said a touch is enough to help. An intimate touch is best— and if my still horny brain can't help but see his thick finger and compare it some of the human dicks I've seen in the past... and admit that, if the claw was gone, it would be a nice size to ride—but I can't let that happen again.

There are countless reasons why, too. And, as I stare down at the inviting water, feeling the weight of his stare on my back, I have to say that not wanting to lead Glaine on... that's one of them.

Which is why, when he says plainly, "I can bathe you," I'm glad he can't see my face.

I don't turn around, though I do shake my head. "I think I can handle this on my own."

He makes a soft sound. "Very well. The chains won't let me leave your side, but I will give you my back. You have my word that I will not look."

Now, I didn't say *that*. I just wasn't ready to hop naked into a bathtub with Glaine after seeing how attracted to him I was earlier. I could blame the mate sickness all I wanted—and I *will*—but what if it washes over me again? If he's naked and my dress is off, will I refuse if he says that oral isn't enough, that I'll need penetration next time?

I know me. I'm not the type to beat around the bush. There's no time for that. I may be cautious when it comes to anything that involves Sierra, but if I'm the only one at risk, I have a tendency to jump in feet-first.

If I decide to sleep with Glaine, I will. So, sorry, but I need to make sure that the temptation isn't there.

Still, I can't stop thinking about the way he said he trusted me. He meant it. If we're in this together for as long as it takes—and we have at least three days ahead of us—maybe... maybe I can trust him a little, too.

"I can wash myself," I tell him, turning slightly so that I can see the flat expression on his face, "but if you want to keep me company, I'm okay with that."

The flat expression cracks. He's so careful to shield himself, too, that at the first hint of rejection, the grumpy guard shuts down. But when I make that suggestion... I see the hunger return.

"I would very much like to do that."

I shrug, ignoring the heat rushing through my veins; as hot as Sombra is, this is even *hotter*. Then, because I can't completely remove my dress due to the chains, I shimmy it up and over my head, letting it settle on the links between me and Glaine.

He sucks in a breath. His eyes go impossibly green, and it suddenly hits me that I didn't get the chance to see his reaction to my naked pussy earlier. I was a little too distracted with the sensation of his hot mouth on my skin to see if he was disgusted—or intrigued.

Looking at his reaction now? I'm going with *entranced.*

"Billie," he rumbles, flexing his claws as if dying to reach out for me... and barely restraining himself. "I wondered... but now I see. My mortal mate, you are absolutely beautiful."

He means it—and the way my stomach flips again, I know that I'm in more trouble now than when I thought I was trapped in that dungeon.

CHAPTER 13
IN NUIT

BILLIE

What a letdown.

And I don't mean the bath. The warm water does enough to help me relax for the first time in, well, a *long* time. It's magic, too. Once all the ash runs from my skin, turning the water a dingy grey, it starts to heat up. It doesn't disappear—since I didn't see a drain or a spout, I don't even know how any of this was possible—but it turns clear, with an added hint of a spicy smelling soap to help me freshen up.

I even let Glaine use his claws to gently scrub the ash out of my hair. And though the magic ends there, and I have to wait for my curls to air dry without any product to style them, I feel a million times better after that.

But when our time together in that room was over…

Total letdown.

I shouldn't complain. After two days of monotonous travel that got broken up by a demon challenge and the best head I've ever received, it was actually nice to sleep in a real bed for the next couple of nights—or 'moons' as the Sombra demons refer to it.

We get to eat. I try demon wine, then swap it for regular water when it makes me woozy and light-headed. I flirt with Glaine because, well, demon wine.

I wait for the doppelseers to see if his future's changed—or what they've seen about mine.

They won't explain anything other than that they need to be surrounded by our essence to see and to understand, and that Glaine should know better than to tempt Fate.

And because I refuse to use his essence to find out what that means, I have no clue what to make of that.

I asked him. I wheedled him. He gave me vague details about his time in the doppelseers' cabin nearly *seven hundred years* ago, but I kinda got a little side-tracked at the thought of Glaine doing anything *seven hundred freaking years* ago.

Still, I now know he had a prophecy from each of

the twins when he was much younger. Over time, part of it's come to pass... and not in a good way. Murmuring softly while staring unblinkingly at me, he solemnly says he's still holding out hope that he might have a better future ahead of him, but because I won't do what's expected of a Sombra demon's mate and pry into his essence myself, we're at an impasse.

Especially when, after three days, the only thing that's said in front of me again as our invitation is suddenly revoked after breakfast is a plain statement by Lucian:

Nothing has changed. The course is straight, though the path may be bumpy.

I want to argue—or ask them for details—but Glaine thanks the doppelseers for their hospitality and ushers me out the door while I'm still cursing at them in English for wasting my time. I mean, talk about rude. Right when I was getting used to demon comfort —and Glaine's presence in the room we shared— Lucian made it clear to Glaine that they were ready to move on, too.

Pity that they don't offer us a ride to Nuit. Maybe if I hadn't snapped and lost my temper, they might have; or maybe, since I don't understand the magic behind their moving cabin—and Glaine just respects it—it wouldn't have worked. Whatever. I'm grateful enough for the rest and that we didn't have to look over our shoulders while we were there, even if I'd secretly hoped that they might be testing me and prove to be powerful enough to get rid of these damn chains after all.

Oh, no. We need a mage for that, not a seer, and Glaine is still sure that we'll find one willing to help us in this Nuit place.

For once, I appreciate his open arrogance. He can't imagine why anyone would refuse to help him if he traveled all the way to see them. It's like he's sure that they'd be thrilled at the honor to defy the duke and help a pair of fugitives, if only because Glaine is one of them.

The three days we spent in the upstairs of the doppelseers' cabin gave me a better insight to him; that, and the snippets of his essence that not even my stubborn ass could block out. Once I start to realize that, as the head of the demon duke's guard, Glaine is actually pretty well-known in this world, I start to see shades of Sierra in his attitude. That slight sense of entitlement that my best friend would deny if I called her out on it, but only because she's so used to being the most famous person in the room, she's become sort of numb to her privilege. Almost like she expects people to jump because she's Whiskey Rose. I love her, and I know it's more than fifteen years in the biz that warped her, but it's true.

Once I understand that Glaine's the way he is because of his prestige and power—and the sudden loss of them when he joined me in Duke Haures's dungeon—I start to understand him more.

I start to like him more.

And I start to wonder if it would be so bad if the mate sickness rears its ugly head again...

It hasn't yet, but the way Glaine keeps shooting me heated glances, I can tell he's waiting for some sign of the mate sickness to hit me so that he can be there to ease it in a way more intimate than just brushing our skin together.

On the plus side, the demon twins gave Glaine their solemn agreement that they will continue to use their magic to conceal us until we reach Nuit. After that, we're on our own. Since I plan on getting a one-way ticket out of here as soon as I get my hands on Glaine's mage friend, I'm not worried about it.

But the lingering mate sickness that bothers me on the last leg of our journey? That's a totally different story...

At first, I ignore it. I'm so eager to reach the demon village that I can pretend it isn't there. Only one problem: I'm a sexual creature. I always have been. I like sex. It's fun, it feels good, and it helps me relieve the stresses of the day. No denying that, since I've been in Sombra, I've been nothing but stressed. True, that's my default state when I'm as busy as I am, but throw in the mate sickness and my growing attraction to Glaine now that I don't hate his guts as much...

I blame the stupid essence. I don't want to commiserate with my demon kidnapper, but now that I know his thoughts, his feelings, and his motives… I can't help but feel sorry for him that, in all the worlds, he got stuck with me as his one true mate.

Demons recognize their mates. I might not understand it, and I definitely don't like it, but I *am* his fated mate. It won't be official until I agree and bond myself to him, but that doesn't change the fact that we have this tie between us that is getting harder and harder to ignore.

Especially when I'm struggling to resist the urge to strip off my dress and jump the big demon.

At that thought, another wave of need washes over me. I sigh and, flexing my fingers in a grabby motion, I gesture at Glaine.

Without a word, he takes his hand in mine. It helps. Could be better, but at least I'm not slyly trying to rub my legs together as I walk.

Glaine squeezes my fingers. "You need your male."

"I need a vibrator," I mutter.

Okay. Sexual frustration makes me bitter. Since we've figured out how to handle the mate sickness without Glaine putting his mouth on me—which isn't a shame at all, no, *really*—by occasionally holding hands to keep it at bay, I've been okay. There's no reason to get any more involved at this point.

Now, if I thought I could sleep with him and he'd

only accept that it was for release and nothing else like before, I'd be desperate enough to see if we fit. But we can't, though the constant empty ache down below is beginning to piss me off.

He can tell.

Glaine tilts his head, looking down at me with a confused expression. Using his free hand, he gestures below. "Why would you require a false cock when I have one that's meant only for you?"

I squeeze my thighs together at the reminder that he's a virgin who would remedy that with me the second I give him the chance. "Why? Because plastic doesn't get attached."

He shakes the chains with the hand still holding mine. "We cannot be more attached." His green eyes glimmer. "Unless, of course, you welcome my cock in your cunt."

I can't help it. I laugh. "When did you get so bold?"

His chest puffs up in pride that he was able to make me chuckle. "When I understood that my mate is no shy, coquettish mortal. She is equally bold and appreciates a male who tells her what it is he wants."

"That's never been your problem, Glaine. You've made it clear from the beginning what it is *you* want."

"Very true," he allows. "But in case you need the reminder, I am here to give it."

The reminder that he's dying to fuck me? Yup. I think I got the message on that one all right.

It doesn't matter. It doesn't matter how much he wants me, or how I'm growing more and more curious by the hour. It would be cruel to sleep with him, then turn around and leave. And since Glaine has promised me that we're quickly approaching Nuit... if I'm lucky, I should be back in Manhattan by the end of the day.

I push down the slight pang of disappointment that hits me when I think that. It has to be coming from Glaine, right? I mean, I *have* to go home. I can't just give up my whole life to have a fling with my demon kidnapper, especially since he's definitely not the 'fling' type. He wants a forever mate. Full stop. He still thinks that's me, and while having his essence has certainly shaken my belief that it can't be possible... it doesn't matter if it is.

I'm going home and nothing can change that.

Of course, those might just be my famous last words...

"Yeah, well, thanks for the offer. And for helping take the edge off." I flex my fingers again, our sign that I'm done with letting him hold my hand. "It helped."

"I know something that will help more," he says in a low voice.

I'm sure he does. "Thanks, but pass."

He sighs. "It is for the best. My Billie is bold, but whether she minds if someone sees her with her male or not, I won't stand for it. Her pleasure is for me alone."

Huh? I'm about to ask him where that possessive edge came from when, suddenly, he points with his free hand.

For a heartbeat, I freeze. I see a shadowy figure in the distance and am immediately thrown back to the rogue demon stalking us. Only Glaine lifts his hand high in a gesture of greeting, and the other figure matches it.

I look over at Glaine. "You know him?"

"Look over there, my Billie. Do you see how he has two pairs of horns?"

I squint. It's hard to make out shadows on top of shadows, though I'm getting better, and it takes me a moment to see what he's referring to.

"Uh. Yeah. I think so."

"Only one demon in Nuit is a two-horn," he explains. "That is Loki."

Loki... excitement fills my chest. "The mage?"

He nods, nowhere near as excited as I am. "Yes. He must've used magic to sense our approach. That, or the doppelseers' protection ended and he knew to expect us. Either way, just beyond those shadows is Nuit."

We *made* it.

This time, I take Glaine's hand instead of waiting for him to take mine. "Let's go."

If I thought Glaine is a grump, Loki is worse. He glares at me the entire time Glaine explains why we journeyed all this way to see him. It started when he glanced at our hands, noticing that we were connected, and it only got worse when he took in the chains.

I held my breath, sure he would refuse. But he doesn't. All Glaine has to tell him is that I am his mate—and when I don't deny it like I did back at the duke's palace, Loki sees no reason why we should still be wearing the gold chains.

Without anything more than a nod and his purple eyes flaring brightly for a split second, he disappears them.

"I thank you, Loki," Glaine begins, pausing when the demon mage interrupts him with a sound. Loki clears his throat, then waves his hand near his horns while purposely staring at Glaine.

I follow his stare just in time to see him reach up to stroke one of his own—

I do a double-take. He's stroking one of his horns, but he has *four*. Like Loki, Glaine has two pairs. There's the one set that I'm familiar with; starting a few inches past his hairline, curving back and over his crown. Another starts at his hairline before jutting straight up.

Where did *they* come from?

Despite not wanting to rely on Glaine's essence too much, there are some things that I just know now. Like how demons are immortal. In their shadowy shapes, it's hard to hurt them. If something wounds them when they're solid, they can turn to mist and back again, healing up their injury in no time. But not horns, it seems. Like that lost demon who tried to challenge Glaine for me that broke his horn in the fight, if we hadn't had to put him down, it would've taken his horn ages to grow back.

But Glaine... the second the chains were finally removed from us, he sprouted a second pair as it was no big deal.

Then, to my stunned surprise, he acts the same as he says plainly to the other demon, "It's fine. I have my sword. I will shear them off later."

Wait. What?

"Glaine?"

He smiles indulgently at me, then turns back to Loki. "I'm glad you came to meet us at the clan's borders. But I must ask... where is Apollyon?"

"And Lilith?" asks Loki.

Glaine jerks his head in a nod.

I glance at him out of the corner of my eye. I... whoa. Something even weirder just happened. Just hearing that unfamiliar name has my heart jolting, then sinking. A fleeting ache dashes through me, there and gone again, leaving the impression that she's hurt me.

Well, not me. *Glaine.*

Lilith? Who is Lilith?

Now, I don't talk about my past lovers. If he wants to torture himself and dip into my memories, watching me with any other guy I've been with, that's on him. I'm not shy. I don't regret anything I've done, even if I wish I was a better judge of character. Knowing that my whole relationship with Trevor was a farce pisses me off, but I was a willing participant in it until he dropped the bomb on me. But just because I'm not a prude, that doesn't mean I kiss and tell.

That's part of the reason the whole essence exchange bothered me at first. To demons, it's natural. It's part of their mating tradition. Humans are used to being alone in their own heads. We have a certain degree of privacy we're used to. So I try not to sneak peeks at Glaine's past in the hope that he stays out of mine.

I use it to be able to understand the world around me, that's all. From understanding Sombran to knowing that a white-eyed demon can be demonic—or a visionary—and all the other rules in Sombra that are commonplace to everyone but me. I'm okay with Glaine getting his English download and reading my emotions so that I don't have to waste my time explaining how I'm feeling.

Right now, though? I'm feeling… odd.

Shit. I'm feeling *jealous*.

I'm sure, if I search, I can get the answer to my question. Glaine obviously knows Lilith, and whatever happened between him and this other demon... demoness... will be in his memories. However, that would make me the worst kind of hypocrite if I looked. It's his business. If he wanted me to know about Lilith, he would've told me on our long journey to Nuit.

Something tells me that he *doesn't* want me to know...

One thing for sure: she can't be his former lover. For good or for bad, I'm the only one he's ever had, and we haven't even fully fucked yet. I let him give me oral, and that's when he told me that he'd never been intimate with anyone else before.

But when I hear Lilith's name, I get the distinct impression that he wanted to be with her.

Whatever. Everyone has a past, and I can't act like his bothers me. Not when he thinks I'm his future and he doesn't get that I can't be.

So when Loki's purple gaze darts over me before he says, "The clan leader and clanmother could sense your approach... and your mortal's. They allowed me to meet you at the edge of Nuit first because of Kennedy," I twist a curl around my finger idly, acting as though all of this doesn't interest me in the slightest.

Does he buy it? Does it matter?

Ugh.

Either way, Glaine lets it go.

"I'm sure I will see him soon enough," he says. "Just

like I'm assuming that, since he sent you to greet us, I haven't been banished from Nuit."

For a second, I don't know why he would be—and then I remember. Technically we're fugitives from the duke's dungeon, aren't we?

I wait to see how Loki will respond. If he knows we're trouble—and the chains were a big clue, I bet—then he might kick us out, leaving me to have to look for another mage.

Only he doesn't. Instead, he simply says, "You are welcome."

Glaine bows his head. "Then I would like to take my mate to my quarters."

Loki nods, then turns, leading the way back into the village. "Of course. And—" His head snaps up, nostrils flaring as he tilts his head to the left. "My Kennedy? I know you are there."

"Sorry, Loki," comes a sweet voice that doesn't sound a little bit apologetic. "But I haven't seen another human mate since Hope and I was curious—"

Wait. Human mate?

That voice... it isn't Glaine's essence translating Sombran to English for me. It's *actually* someone speaking my language.

Excitement mingled with homesickness rushes through me as someone steps out from behind the nearest structure.

CHAPTER 14

KENNEDY... AND LILITH

BILLIE

It's definitely a human woman. She has a heart-shaped face, dark blonde hair that falls down her shoulder, and a pair of big, brown eyes.

Oh, and she's visibly pregnant.

Is that what I have to look forward to if I decide to throw caution to the wind and continue this adventure in Sombra? Accept Glaine as my mate and start popping out half-demon, half-human babies while he keeps me pregnant and barefoot in the demon version of a kitchen I can't use?

I chuckle wryly as I look down at my ash-covered feet. Looks like I got the barefoot part down pat, I think, before looking up to see that, while I might've been staring at her belly before, she's now gaping at *me*.

Okay. I know I'm a hot mess. I got spoiled at the doppelseers, but they obviously didn't have any curly girl products. Plus my poor dress is trash.

But is it really that bad—

"Oh my God! You're Billie! From Thr33peat." She cocks out her hip, showing off the slight bump of her belly as she strikes a very familiar pose. "'One, Two, Three'," she sings out, managing to match my contralto voice, Tandy's soprano, and Sierra's signature rasp in the way she calls out each of our ridiculous stage names. She goes from high to low—just like we did— waggling her finger a little when she gets to Sierra's 'Three' before she straightens, cradling that same bump. "You're Two!"

I've run into fans in the strangest of places. Nothing weirder than having a woman about your age start singing one of your fifteen-year-old hits while you're awkwardly folding your panties in a laundromat, I'll tell you that, but I've learned to take it all in stride. When it's between having someone recognize me randomly or having a face that everyone on Earth knows, I'll take a handful of weekly encounters while still living my life over being trapped in her own fame like my best friend.

Does that mean I expect to find a Thr33peat fan in *Sombra*? It was one thing for Glaine to tell me that there are a handful of human mates who live in his realm. He's immortal. Time runs differently here. I just never thought that the first one I'd run into would not only be my contemporary, but also the right age to be into my girl group during our heyday.

"I prefer Billie." My voice is firm, but I temper it with a smile.

"I'm Kennedy. Wow. I was a huge fan growing up. I was crushed when you guys broke up, but... hang on. Do you still know Whiskey Rose?"

My smile doesn't waver. This is pretty common, too. The second anyone puts two and two together—or Two and Three—and realizes that my former bandmate is one of the most popular performers in the world, they inevitably wonder if we kept in touch. That's why it was such a big thing when I went to the *Jessica's Journey* premiere with Sierra before Patrick Ridgefield opened fire. If only for one night, I stepped back into the limelight beside Sierra instead of standing behind her.

Kennedy. Suddenly part of what Loki said makes sense. The demons in charge passed on the responsibility of me and Glaine to Loki because he has a human mate.

A *pregnant* human mate.

A pregnant human mate who couldn't have been here too long if she knows about Whiskey Rose...

"I do," I say. "I actually manage her these days."

"That's awesome! I'd love to meet her." You and me both, sister. "She's my favorite singer. I even have all of her records downloaded on this mp3 player Shannon brought me. It's like my Kindle. I can have all my favorite songs and books here in Sombra for when I miss being in the human world."

Loki's purple eyes flash, a hint of white overtaking the violet shade for a heartbeat. As though he's completely forgotten about me and Glaine, he moves in on his mate. "My Kennedy," he murmurs. "I want nothing more than for you to be happy and content with your male here."

"I am. You know I am. Maybe not at first," she admits, and the look she tosses my way makes me think I have a *ton* more questions for Kennedy, "but I love you, Loki. You know that."

"You are my heart," he rumbles, taking her hands gently in his, pulling her into his embrace. "My everything."

Loki bows his head over his mate, pressing his forehead to Kennedy's, his double pair of horns just skimming the top of her crown as she murmurs something softly in response to her mate.

Purposely ignoring their display of public affection, I grab Glaine by the forearm, dragging him to the side so that we're not overhead. And, yes, I know he only comes with me because he wants to, not that I can actually make him go anywhere, but still. "Aren't you going to ask him about the travel spell? So I can go back home?"

Glaine's lips thin. For a split second there, I'm sure he's going to remind me that I'm his mate, and that despite his implied promise to get me out of the dungeon, then help me return to New York, he changed his mind… but then he sighs.

"I will, Billie. He already did more than he should, removing the chains before he spoke to Apollyon and got his permission to interfere. Let's wait until tomorrow. We'll know more then."

Tomorrow. I can wait until tomorrow.

"But what about now?"

If given the choice, I'd rather not watch the happily bonded couple coo at each other. I also don't think I want to hear Kennedy fawn over Sierra anymore. I'm sure I'll have that to look forward to it if I bump into Kennedy again before we go—and, if I want her mate to do me a favor, I need to be nice to her—but for now… yeah. I'm okay.

We're not chained together anymore, but that doesn't mean that Glaine is ready to give up our connection. Moving his hand, shifting it so that mine falls from his forearm, he takes my fingers in his. His hand swallows mine up, but he holds it as best he can, turning the tips of his claws to shadow so that he doesn't accidentally jab me.

"Now? I take you home."

I'm so excited about finding a place to sit, to rest, to get *clean* that I don't even point out that it's *his* home, not mine.

Nuit is just what I think of when I hear the term 'village'. From what I understand, there are countless communities in Sombra, each one nestled together with a communal area known as the village square. There are houses that remind me of squat condos built side-by-side in a large circle, providing a border that protects the demons from any of the threats that lurk in Sombra's darker shadows.

There are no skyscrapers here. No apartment buildings. Each home is for single demons or mated pairs and their families. A couple have a second floor, though most are a ranch-style with multiple rooms on that ground floor.

Because of his status as a soldier, Glaine has a narrow two-floor home made of burnt wood and magic, similar to the structure where the doppelseers live in their corner of the shadows. The magic provides light and running water; the windowless wood forms shelter from the rest of the village and the oppressive heat.

I don't know why it's cooler inside, only that it is. In Glaine's home, he has a living area that doubles as a dining area, with the table made of the same wood as the house itself. There is a stove in one corner for cooking hot meals, and a box that keeps perishables cold in a way that mimics a refrigerator but it isn't one. It works the same, though, and I'm amazed by how magic in Sombra makes the hellish realm seem so much more advanced than back home.

Take the demon version of a toilet in the assigned 'facilities' room in his place. Sure, it took some getting used to, going in a hole in the ground, but once you drop your waste inside, it simply vanishes. A puff of air and a bidet-like squirt of water cleans you up and dries you off; it's so much more sanitary than toilet paper without having a toilet to scrub when you're done! There's a water basin and soap dispenser for your hands, and a tub even larger than the one the demon twins had.

Despite Glaine admitting it has been quite some time since he returned to Nuit, his home is dust-free—if not ash-free—and nowhere near as musty as I expected. I see why when I go to the second floor. There, in the ceiling, are circular cut-outs like they have in the palace.

He gives me an illustration of their use when I ask. Going from his solid demon form to that mess of shadows, he contracts in on himself before whizzing out of the hole.

Shadow travel, I realize enviously. If it hadn't been

for the chains keeping him from turning transparent like that, maybe we could've cut a couple of days of walking off our journey to Nuit.

When he comes back, he's holding his sword. I don't even get the chance to ask why he is before he's gripping one of the newly generated horns by the tip, raising his sword up to it as if he's about to—

Shear it off.

Oh, hell no.

"What are you doing?"

He pauses, sword still in the air. "Would you rather I go in another room? There won't be any blood when I cut off the horn, if that's what you're worried about."

No. I'm worried about the demon thinking it's perfectly normal to chop off his horns. "Why would you do that? You just got them back. If it takes centuries to grow... why would you want to get rid of them?"

Glaine sucks in a breath, lowering the sword as if realizing that I have major concerns about this. "My horns are different. It's not like losing one in a challenge. These are my second horns. Every few times I turn to my shadows and back, they reappear and I must get rid of them."

"Why?"

He doesn't answer me. Because he wants me to see for myself in his essence?

Too bad.

I try another tactic. "Does it hurt?"

"I've grown used to it over the centuries."

That's not a no. "Why would you hurt yourself? I don't get it. And," I add, jabbing my pointer finger at him when he opens his mouth, "I don't want you to say that I could tell from your essence. That's not the point. I'm asking *you*."

Glaine sighs. "There are... expectations of two-horns. Expectations that I'd rather not deal with."

"Like?"

Before he can answer me, we're interrupted by a loud knock at the door, so strong it reaches us upstairs.

"Someone is at the door," Glaine announces needlessly.

No shit.

"Would it be rude to ignore them?" I ask.

I already know the answer before he nods. "Yes."

Fine. "Okay. Let's go see who it is. But don't think this topic of conversation is over, Glaine. I don't know why you think it's okay to mutilate yourself, but if Loki can walk around with two pairs of horns, you should, too."

"Loki is a mage."

And? "So? You're a guard. You'd think that having an extra pair of points to threaten the duke's enemies with would be a plus."

He frowns. "It's not that—"

Knock, knock, knock.

The banging has taken on a little more of an urgent edge.

I throw Glaine another look that says we're still not done, mourn the fact that I didn't get the chance to try out the wash basin to clean the ash off my feet just yet, then start for the stairs as soon as I make sure he disappears that sword of his.

The heavy footfalls behind me and the oversized shadow falling in front of me let me know that Glaine is right there.

Once we reach the door, I step aside, letting him open it. After all, this is his home. I'm just being nosy, seeing who could be out there since there are no windows for me to peek through.

Glaine pulls in the door, revealing a Sombra demon male.

From my angle beside my demon, I see that the newcomer is about a half-head shorter than Glaine. Like Glaine, he is in his solid demon form. Unlike Glaine, he's wearing a tan-colored linen shirt, dark brown pants, and black foot coverings.

Glaine's house wasn't too far from where we met Loki, but during our quick walk over, I noticed that the village is different from the palace in so many ways. Mavro is a blue-tinged oasis, unlike the reddish rest of the realm, and the heat and humidity is a bitch. The demons here seem to prefer their solid form instead of the inky black shadows of the mages and guards in the duke's palace, and while some of them wear the same shadow coverings as Glaine—like Loki—others are in real clothes.

This demon has gold eyes instead of green like Glaine, and a firm expression on his deep red face.

Glaine nods at him. "Apollyon. After you weren't there to meet us at the border of the village, I would've thought you'd wait until we'd settled in from our travels before you'd come to see me. We had to go on foot, and it took longer than we expected. We were resting."

Smooth, Glaine. No mention that we broke out of jail, though I'm sure all of Nuit knows by now, and he just about asks the clan leader to give us until tomorrow to figure out our next step before he pulls rank.

No dice.

Apollyon opens his mouth, then gives Glaine a second look when he notices that he probably has an extra pair of horns than he remembers.

I wait to see if the other demon will comment on it, but after taking a moment to compose himself, he lowers his gaze—and I'm even more determined to keep Glaine from lopping them back off.

"I don't want to disturb you and your mate, but it cannot be helped. I must speak to you."

Glaine settles his massive hand on my shoulder. I notice that his skin isn't as scorching to the touch as it used to be, and I don't shake him off as he says, "You will speak to us both."

"Glaine. I've had a message from Duke Haures. I'm sorry, but I think your female should stay behind."

Oh, does he now?

I open my mouth to argue, pausing only when Glaine rubs the side of his thumb along the top of my shoulder blade. It's a gentle yet possessive caress, not a warning to keep from talking, but I do because the big demon is plenty ready to argue on my behalf for me.

"My Billie is an intelligent female with a sharp tongue. Whatever Duke Haures has to say, she should hear it. I'm sure it affects her as much as it does me. I will protect her from all dangers, Apollyon, but I will not belittle her. She doesn't hide. More to the point, where I go, she goes."

Poor Apollyon. He's the head honcho in Nuit, but between Glaine's arrogance and his soldier bearing, you wouldn't be able to tell.

I move my hand down, reaching past Glaine's shadows, squeezing his solid thigh in a show of appreciation. Maybe he's been paying more attention than I thought—or he's a real quick learner when it comes to parsing my essence—because he couldn't have defended me better if he tried.

Apollyon's gold-colored eyes glimmer. "Yes, I understand. But—"

"But," interrupts a female voice, just out of my line

of vision, "you can blame me for this, Glaine. I requested that my mate spirit you off for your conversation so that I could have a moment with the female who seems to have brought the smile back to such a grumpy guard's face."

The big demon jolts in place. I take the opportunity to sidle a little closer, peeking out the open door.

She is as tall as Apollyon, with a similar broad build, but that's where any similarities end. Her skin is a rich golden shade, almost like the other demon's eyes, and she has *orange* hair that she wears in a style that reminds me of Sierra: a thick plait that she has tossed over her shoulder. Instead of shadow coverings like other demons, she follows Apollyon's lead and has on actual clothes: a dress that's woven from brown and white and yellow fabrics, plus a pair of leather-looking boots that I'd give my eyetooth for at this point. The deep brown matches her dainty horns, so much smaller than the male's that it's undeniable that they're more feminine.

The pretty demoness smiles warmly at us both. "Hello, Glaine. Won't you introduce me to your mate?"

It takes a moment for him to react. But, instead of offering this demoness my name, he breathes out hers.

"Lilith."

I go still, the return of my inexplicable jealousy slamming into me so fast, it freezes me in place.

Lilith.

CHAPTER 15
CHITCHAT

BILLIE

Lilith is sitting on the couch in Glaine's living room. I try not to take offense to the fact that I didn't offer her the seat, Glaine did, and that's when Apollyon brought him outside so that the two of them could chat.

I know what's really going on here. Lilith is Apollyon's mate. She's also the female head of the demons who live in Nuit. That makes her in charge, and since Apollyon really doesn't want to talk to Glaine in front of me, she's now my babysitter.

What do they expect? That now that Loki removed the chains from the two of us, I would say 'peace out' and leave Glaine behind in his village. Please. I learned my lesson. It's like hooking up with the right lawyer or venue planner. Stick with the one who can get you further. Leaving Glaine now when I'm so close to getting home... that would be like cutting off my nose to spite my face.

And I have an adorable nose, thank you very much.

It's not fair that I'm being so rude to Lilith for reasons I can't explain. I know that, too. She's been nothing but pleasant after greeting me, and has kept her expression welcoming no matter how much I can't shake this feeling like she means something to me.

Or Glaine.

It would be so tempting to pop into his essence to check. I don't, though. Is it because I have an idea what I'm going to find? Maybe. It's just... it's better to make small talk with the demoness while I wait for him to come back and update me on what the clan leader says.

Because he will. I'm sure of that. For good or for bad, whether it's news I want to hear or not, he'll tell me.

Guys are guys in every world. Maybe... maybe so are ladies.

I can't bring myself to sit on the couch with her, but I do cross my legs at the ankle and lean against the edge of one of the arms. "I really like your dress."

It's not a lie. It's really nice and it flatters her

demoness shape. Plus, it's not a wrinkly mess like my ex-favorite cocktail dress.

"Thank you, Billie. I must introduce you to Raiga. She's the village seamstress. She sews all of Kennedy's dresses, too. I will see that she brings some for you."

I appreciate the offer, but—

"That's not necessary. I won't be staying long."

Her eyes light up. "Oh? So Glaine will be joining you in your realm? That'll be a great loss to Sombra. It is thanks to him and the rest of the duke's guard that this plane has not been overrun by the demons of Brille Rouge. I'd seen the damage they can do in Soleil when I lived there instead of Sombra. He saved many lives in both worlds. We will surely miss him."

We, not I. Does that mean anything? Is that why I sense there is a connection between Glaine and Lilith? Because she's grateful for his service as a soldier, and that they've known each from living in Nuit after she left her demon realm?

Keeping up the light conversational tone, I tell her, "Glaine's staying here."

She furrows her dainty brow. "But he is your mate."

Yeah, well? That remains to be seen.

Barely a week ago, I would've been quick to scoff. At first, I had myself convinced that he had to have mistaken me for Sierra; given the choice between us, almost everyone would choose her, a fact that became undeniable after Trevor's confession. I don't blame her, either. There's a reason the world fell in love with Whiskey Rose, and I've spent years trying to shield her from that as best as I could.

But Glaine never once wavered in his belief that *I* am his mate. From the moment he appeared in our apartment at the Dorado, he's been determined to get me to agree. Barely a week ago, I would've scoffed and said he had no chance. I *did* do that.

But that was a week ago.

Now?

Whatever Damien and Lucian did while we were at the doppelseers' cabin, they planted a seed of doubt. Glaine wants to promise himself to me. After Trevor, I'd been ready to swear off men... but maybe I just needed to narrow it to *human* men. A demon male who is offering me forever, who won't cheat on me or fall in love with my best friend or cast me aside because I'm nothing special?

To Glaine, I *am* special. I'm Billie. I'm *his*—or I could be if I decide to forsake everything I know, everything I have in the human world, and give it all up to stay here with him.

That's what he wants from me. Even if he didn't make that clear right from the start, I have his essence. Though it's pretty obvious he's been able to hide a lot even with the essence exchange, his determination to settle down with his one true mate in Sombra is not one of those things.

And that's the problem right there. Glaine doesn't want to leave Sombra. I've been fascinated by everything I've seen and learned about the demon realm and would love to explore it more... but I'm needed back in New York. Sierra needs me, and I have to go.

When I don't say anything to that, she frowns.

"Glaine loves deeply. He hides it behind his scowl most of the time, but there's a good male beneath the soldier's facade. He will wait as long as it takes."

I know that. Trust me, I *know*.

"You talk about him as if you know him very well," I point out.

"I do."

I figured. "How?"

Lilith's lips quirk into a small smile. "Perhaps that is a conversation best had with your mate."

Oh, don't worry. As soon as Glaine comes back, I'll be having it. Whether it's my business or not, I don't think my curiosity will rest if I don't ask. And using his essence won't work.

I need to hear this straight from Glaine almost as much as I need him to tell me that he's arranged a way back to New York for me.

And if one of those seems a little more urgent to me than the other all of a sudden... I'll deal.

I always deal.

GLAINE

Apollyon paces in front of me, hands folded behind his back. The clan leader has his horns bowed, chin tucked to his chest. We're just outside my home, having left Lilith and Billie together inside. Due to the constraints on a Sombra demon male, I cannot go that far from my mate—a fact that Apollyon recognizes as he keeps his voice low without moving further from the front door.

"You have put me in the most awkward of positions, Glaine," he announces after a few strained moments.

"I didn't mean to, Apollyon."

"I know. Your instincts were at work." He purses his lips, fangs overhanging the bottommost one. "I know that better than other demons. When you see your mate for the first time, you think of nothing else but bonding her to you."

Even if she was being wooed by another male who falsely believed she was his...

That was centuries ago. Any anger I felt toward the clan leader disappeared as soon as Lilith came to me, admitting what we both had sensed in some way: that I was not her mate, Apollyon was, and she was moving from my home to his. She chose him. She recognized him as her fated mate instead of a male who might be, and since she denied giving me her essence or taking mine, she was free to bond with Apollyon.

It hurt to be denied. It was the doppelseers' prophecy come true: that I would find her in another world only for her to refuse me in the end. But now I have Billie—and Lucian confirmed that my fate has not changed.

As for Damien... before I left their cabin with Billie, he spoke to me for the first time. In the same melodic voice as before, he repeated the second prophecy that has ruled my life for so long:

In chains of gold and magic bound,
You linger close, yet far profound.
To win the heart you hold so dear,
Release the spell that chains you here.
For love's true call is not in grasp,
But in the freedom you unfasten at last...

Lucian warned me not to take his twin's riddles so literally. How can I not? For the first time, I understand what it means. *In chains of gold...* he was referring to the chains that kept Billie tethered to me. When I asked her what she wanted of me to prove myself to her, she wanted her freedom. From the dungeon. From the chains. From me.

To win the heart... I used my sway over a younger

demon to earn our escape. I knew Loki would release us from the chains because he has a weakness when it comes to his human mate. To know that I had one... of course he would help me. I didn't ask him to open the travel spell just yet because I was selfish. I wanted to cleave Billie close to me for a little longer.

And now, as Apollyon confesses that Duke Haures sent a messenger to Nuit to speak with him while we were still on our way... I know that I've made another mistake.

My mate wanted her freedom to return to the human realm, but that is the one thing I cannot give her.

"Out of respect for all you've done for Nuit..." He shakes his head, looking away from me. "Out of respect for you bringing Lilith to me, I have agreed to harbor you and your mate. But that means you must stay in Nuit. Both of you."

There's more to the warning. Duke Haures reminds me of the final conversation we shared before he gave his permission for me to join Billie in the dungeon. I'm barely listening since I'm thinking about how I'm going to explain this to my mate, but Apollyon takes my silence as agreement.

Then, ending the conversation quickly, he joins me in my living room. My eyes immediately go to Billie. She's standing in her prickly pose, arms crossed over her chest, legs folded together as she leans against the far wall. Lilith has moved from her place on the couch, putting some distance between her and my human mate.

My *upset* human mate.

Her emotions slam into me like a commander's hand to the back of your horns. She is trying to hide them, but failing, and I know that whatever has passed between the females while Apollyon and I were occupied outside… I had made a mistake by leaving Billie behind. I should've insisted she come with me to speak with Apollyon, even if his words weren't to her liking.

Now? I wait for the clan leader and the clanmother to take leave of my home, then turn, knowing that Billie will have questions for me.

Questions I will do my best to answer.

"Who is Lilith?"

That… that is not the question I expected her to start with. Luckily for me, it is an easy one.

"Apollyon's mate."

Billie uncrosses her arms from over her chest, planting them on her hips instead. "Glaine. Please. Don't insult me. I don't want to use your essence because… I don't know. It just seems like a huge invasion of privacy—"

"It's not," I assure her. "Mates… we're meant to know everything about each other. That way there's no doubt that we've chosen the right partner. You are my mate, Billie, and you deserve my essence. That, like everything I have, belongs to you."

My heart is in your hands...

"I get that," she says, and while her essence tells me that she does, there is still much I don't know about my mate. She seems... upset that I left her with Lilith. Not because I left her, but because the other female was there at all.

Maybe it is not as easy a question to answer as I thought.

"I hope you didn't mind that I had to leave to speak with Apollyon," I begin. I wave toward the door. "I didn't go far." I cannot unless I want to burn. "I was right there. I hope... I hope Lilith was kind to you."

Billie snorts. "You know her better than me. Why wouldn't she be kind?"

"Was she?"

"Yeah. She was nice. Offered to get me a couple of dresses if I'll be staying with you for a while—"

I shouldn't be jealous of Lilith. She has a mate, and I know that she is only acting as the clanmother, welcoming Billie to Nuit. But *I* am Billie's male. If she needs new coverings, I will provide them. Now that I can access my shadows, I can clothe her in them if need be; soldiers often weave entire uniforms out of their shadows when they won't be in their solid form for long so I have the skill. If not, I can get them for my mortal.

"Whatever you need, ask me. I will make sure you have it."

I mean it earnestly. I've made my mistakes. Our mating... I started it wrong. I accept that. Apollyon's message from Duke Haures doesn't change anything. I brought Billie to Nuit so that we could find a mage I trusted to remove the chains. I had every intention of asking Loki for a travel spell. If the doppelseers concealed us on our journey, they could do the same if I followed Billie to the human realm to woo her there.

I can't do that now. Duke Haures will be watching the pathways, and if I leave, I will be dragged back in chains. And because of his first law and the fact that Billie has my essence but we are not bonded, he won't stand to let her go, either.

I've gotten exactly what I wanted, and I feel terrible for it.

The sensation only grows when Billie says, "Ask you? Okay. Flat out, then. Are you in love with Lilith?"

I lift my hands, laying my claws over my chest. "I love you, my mortal."

She makes that scoffing sound again. "My fault for giving you the opportunity... let me try again. Were you in love with Lilith?"

I love my mate. That is what Sombra demon males are born to do. Did I believe myself to love Lilith?

My mate will appreciate my honesty. As though I have any other choice. I will never lie to Billie, even if she doesn't like what my answers are, and I sense that —no matter how she acts as though we are *not* mates, even after she let me taste her cunt and touch her to ward off the mate sickness—she will not like it when I say, "When I believed Lilith was meant to be my mate, yes. I loved her. But she is not, and while I am still fond of her, I do not love her now."

BILLIE

Well, I asked, didn't I?

Worse, when I don't respond to his confession, Glaine launches into an explanation revolving around his history with Lilith. How, on a campaign to a neighboring demon plan called Soleil, he met Lilith. He was drawn to her, and she was tired of living in the female-heavy demon realm, so when he offered to bring her to Sombra and allow him to prove he could be a worthy mate, she agreed.

Offered, I notice. Not stole. *Offered.*

He offered her the chance to choose him, too. But Lilith, shortly after settling into Nuit with him, met Apollyon and the rest is history. Like me, she was careful to keep Glaine at arms-length. In her case, she knew she wasn't his mate. In mine, I'm worried that I *am*, and that no matter what, his Fate will trump my human free will.

And I'm terrified that I'll let it.

The jealousy doesn't help. The earnestness in his tone makes any doubt he might be making this all up disappear, and I have to admit that I think I suspected as much. From the jolt that hit him when he first realized Lilith was on the porch all the way back to comments he made, plus the way the doppelseers told him his prophecy still stands as though he'd had reason to doubt it...

Lucian had a vision that boils down to Glaine finding his mate off-plane and her denying him. I just thought he was referring to me because, well, obviously. But the way he is so determined to make me his mate *and* for me to accept him instead of refusing him... I should've guessed he had trauma.

Moving a demoness from another world to his home, so certain that she must be his one true mate only for her to basically give him the 'I just see you as a friend' speech before marrying his friend? Yup. Trauma.

Now, does that mean it was fair of him to take it out on me? At least, with Lilith, he asked her to move to Sombra with him and, for whatever reason she had at the time, she agreed. She clearly knew he wasn't her fated mate. She didn't give her essence to him or take his in return; I know that instinctively as the belief pops into my head, just like Glaine's essence informs me that demons only have one chance to create a bond. So even if he wasn't absolutely sure I'm his, now that I have his essence, if I tell him to kick rocks, I'm basically resigning him to a lonely existence.

Great. As if I need *that* pressure on my shoulders.

See? This is why I need to keep out of Glaine's head and his emotions. What do I care that he thought Lilith was his mate before me? He stole me... it shouldn't bother me at all that he manipulated me into giving him my essence, then taking his. If he never has a mate again, that's not my problem.

But I do care. More than I should—but not enough to make me forget the reason why I came to Nuit with Glaine.

"Forget it. That's enough about my chat with Lilith—"

"Billie. If there's something—"

Nope. "I said that's enough. Moving on. You talked to Apollyon, right? Is everything okay?"

The big demon winces.

Shit.

So... not okay, then.

Moving on.

"Loki," I say, grasping at straws.

Glaine's expression closes off. "Yes? What about him?"

"Loki is a mage. He got rid of the chains."

"Yes."

"Did you ask him? Or Apollyon, I guess. Can he do it? Can he use magic to send me home?"

Glaine tightens his jaw, his oversized fangs digging into the skin beneath his bottom lip as he clenches his teeth.

I get my answer in his reaction—and I don't accept it.

"There's got to be a way."

"Loki serves Duke Haures," Glaine says after a moment. "Apollyon is a fair clan leader, but he also is loyal to the throne."

How much do you want to bet that's a roundabout way of saying that they're too afraid of repercussions from the demon duke to help me?

"This is the clan I was born into," Glaine adds. "I have a home in Nuit because of it, but also centuries of service to Duke Haures in Mavro. Before we arrived, he sent a messenger on the assumption I would take you here with me. His grace, in his mercy, has decided not to punish us for escaping the dungeon and the chains—"

"What? That's great—"

Glaine's expression gentles. "—but he has decreed that no one is to cast a travel spell from Sombra to the human realm for me again. I've lost his trust, and my position as his top soldier. I am exiled to Nuit. Just Nuit. My privilege to go off-plane has been revoked." His nostrils flare. "As has yours unless my clever female finds a way around his command."

No doubt Glaine has been looking at my memories and seeing all of the contracts that I negotiated on Sierra's behalf—and how often I kept either one of us from being trapped in a shitty situation even worse than this.

Sierra... Whether my best friend really is in this mess up to her eyeballs like I am, I don't know, and without finding a way back to New York to see her again, I'm not sure I ever will. One thing for sure, though? The chains are gone, but I'm still not free.

And, because of me, neither is Glaine.

Worse, I got him *fired.*

That's the modern way of thinking of it. It's probably ten times worse for Glaine. Hundreds if I think about how many years he served as a member of Duke Haures's guard. He worked his way to the top, taking the position as lead soldier all so he would be poised to go after the one thing he wanted most: a mate. That's what led him to Lilith, and when that wasn't the happy ending he was after, he stumbled on me.

What was it he told me that first night in the dungeon? It was a promise. No. A *vow*—

I will do whatever I must to show you that I will be a

good and honorable and devoted mate to you. Ask for anything in my power, female, and it is yours.

I wanted out of the cell. He broke me out.

I wanted to go home... and he tried. I'll give him credit. He *tried.*

But it didn't work.

My mouth goes dry. I dart out my tongue, dabbing at my lower lip. "So we're still being punished."

The look on his face now says that Glaine doesn't *not* agree. "It's the first law for a reason, Billie. We're not bonded. You have my essence... Duke Haures cannot allow you to return to the human realm to tell stories about my people."

"But—"

"You are an honest female. If you gave me your word that you'd keep the secret, I'd believe you."

"Let me guess. And the duke wouldn't?"

He nods his head.

I purse my lips, then blurt out, "I still want to know what the deal with the second pair of horns is."

If he thinks my change of subject is sudden, he doesn't say anything about it. Probably because he's expecting me to, like, break down or something because he's just confirmed my worst suspicions: I'm stuck here. Our Hail Mary didn't come to pass. We got the chains off, but that's about it. For now, at least, I'm not going home.

That sucks. I mean it. I was living in denial these

last few days, convinced that things would work out because I wanted them to. I know better. To get what you want, you have to earn it. I'll find a way home eventually. That won't be the last New York sees of me because I refuse to never see Sierra again.

But if what Glaine suspects is true... I will. Sooner or later. For now? I'm not gonna cry. I'm gonna do what I always do: *deal with it.*

I have Glaine. There's that. Against my better judgment, I've grown fond of the demon. Amazing, really, when I think about how pissed I was that he grabbed me and brought me to Sombra. Even though I've been trying not to rely on his essence, sometimes it just happens. I know him better now. *Understand* him better.

He just wanted his true love.

He thought that was Lilith once, but she broke his heart. For centuries after, he hardened it, hiding that pain behind a glower and a sense of duty to the duke. He did what he was told, and when he stumbled upon who he believes is his *real* mate? Can I blame him for acting as impulsively as he did when it was his instincts in control?

For a moment, I think he's going to refuse to tell me. That, or change the subject himself.

He doesn't.

"Sombra demons born with a second pair of horns are known as two-horns. I'm sure you noticed that Loki is a two-horn. They're almost always born as mages, too, their second horns giving them increased power. But for a soldier to bear that mark... I knew from a young age I would never rise up the ranks of the duke's commands with them, so I got rid of them."

I look at the two pairs of horns. He went to such lengths to be the perfect soldier. Cutting off the extra pair every time they regenerated so that he wouldn't lose his post... and after all that, the duke tossed him in the dungeon because of his attachment to me. And now he's released him from his guard.

I will do whatever I must to show you...

In his own way, he has, hasn't he? He's lost his job. His standing with the duke. His position in this world... and he's done it all for me.

And what have I done? Reminded him at every turn that I'm desperate to get away from him. That all I want is to go home. I never even thought about how much he was giving up, knowing that I was repaying him for stealing me without my permission by using him to go home, no matter what it cost him in the end.

He wanted to prove himself. I never gave him the chance.

Well, I can now... I mean. What do I have to lose? And if his 'clever mate' can figure out a way around Duke Haures's command... who knows? I traveled through Sombra with Glaine. He can turn to shadows now. Maybe he wants to check out Manhattan.

It's a thought, and I'm still thinking it as Glaine reaches up, stroking the front horn.

"Do you like them?"

He draws me back to the conversation with his deep, rumbling voice.

"I— what?"

"The two-horns. There are those in Nuit who existed when I was a mere spawn. They'd remember a time before I started to hide them any way I could. Magic. Breaking them in reckless challenges. Then, later, with the sword gifted to me by Duke Haures when I was still a favored guard."

He adds that last part, not to guilt-trip me, but because it's been part of his identity for so long, he can't help it. Just like he's used to hiding a part of himself.

"For those who don't, it will draw attention. They will wonder if I have magic that I do not, or if being a two-horn fated soldier"—because of his green eyes— "means that I am more bloodthirsty than others. It might be better if I sheared them, but if you like them..."

"I do."

"Then I shall keep them."

"You don't have to do that just because I said so," I argue.

Glaine looks down at me, his unblinking stare showing more emotion than I'm sensing vaguely from his essence. "I know. But if it pleases you, my mate, I will."

And though he doesn't say it, I hear the promise all the same.

I will do anything for you.

A WEEK PASSES IN SOMBRA, AND WHILE I REFUSE TO GIVE up all hope, with the choice of being able to return to Manhattan completely out of my hands, I find myself acclimating as best I can.

What makes it easier? Is how Glaine holds true to his word.

I guess it helps that I let down my guard a little, too. He's given me a place to stay. He makes sure I'm fed, that I'm dressed, and that I'm comfortable. When he sees the way I ooh and ahh over Kennedy's strange little pet, he offers to bring me to the edge of the Nuit so that he can catch me an ungez of my own to replace Three. It's a little too soon—especially when I think of what happened to poor Two—but I appreciate the gesture.

We're getting along. Better than I expected, too. We have our arguments, especially when he tries to tell me what to do and I make it clear I won't tolerate that, but since he's learned to let me win when it counts... I'm actually beginning to like my demon.

Okay. I admit it. Without the pathway back to New York opening for me as easily as I hoped, I started to wonder *what if*. What if this was meant to happen? What if Glaine is right about me being the one true mate he's waited centuries for? What if I make the best of a weird situation and stick around? That way it's now *my* choice.

So maybe Fate got her hooks in me. Maybe I'm giving in too easily.

Or maybe I just really, really need to get laid.

That's part of it. We've managed to keep the mate sickness under control since we've been in Nuit. I notice that, once I start thinking of Glaine as my mate, it's not so bad. Kinda like the ache and the need was that bad because the Sombra demon gods were punishing me for ignoring them. Once I start thinking 'maybe', they give me a little break to get my head— and my heart—in order.

Does that mean I'm ready to make this official with him? No. I'm not that far gone, but the longer we're in Sombra together, the more I'm thinking about taking things a little further.

That's one thing I can say about Glaine. It took two nights before I could get him to agree to sleep in the same bed as me. Luckily, it's so much bigger than the cot in the dungeon, and if I subconsciously know it's because it was built with Glaine and his demoness mate in mind, I flick that tiny tidbit far, far away. It fits us comfortably, which works for me. But though we lie next to each other and Glaine eventually ends up spooning me, protecting me even on the rare occasion he sleeps himself, he hasn't made a single move. I can't stop thinking about how strong he is and how he lifted me up like I was a doll before making me come harder than I ever have before, and he doesn't even pretend to accidentally cop a feel.

I'd appreciate how much he respects me if I wasn't going out of my head with lust for my demon.

Normally, when I was stuck like this, I would go to Sierra for help. It wasn't often. I usually had no trouble being decisive and knowing what I wanted to do without bothering her busy schedule, but I always knew that she'd make time for me if I needed it. In Sombra, my options are limited. Going to Lilith for advice is out.

Good thing I have Kennedy.

She's curled up on the couch with me. Freya, her pet ungez, is sitting on her shoulders while Kennedy absently rubs her growing belly. I'm on the other end, legs up to my chest, arms wrapped around them as she tells me everything I can expect about demon sex.

Turns out, humans and demons do fit. It's a tight squeeze at first, but just like how the gods chose me for Glaine for a reason, when the time comes, our physical differences don't really matter. And if they do? Like, say

I was a virgin and that was the first dick I ever had? There are ways around it.

I'm not too concerned. I've seen Glaine naked; he's not all that shy, either, especially after he bathes and before he conjures his shadow clothing. That's all the more reason why I'm thinking about this as hard as I am. He looks good naked, and the first time he walked across the room after his bath, I was already trying to figure out if it would be worth a try.

He's long. Not too thick. It's a lot, but considering I had a fling with a bonafide well-hung porn star in my early twenties, I'm pretty sure I can handle it. If I can't? Kennedy tells me that all I have to do is ask Glaine to turn that part of his anatomy to shadow. Not only will we fit easier, but it's supposed to feel *amazing*.

I only have one question that has me holding off.

"But what if I do sleep with him? Won't that finish the bond?"

I get the answer from Glaine's essence almost the same time as Kennedy says, "Nah. Trust me. I didn't want to get stuck here either when Loki made off with me. But because sometimes the body knows before the heart does, I had sex with him way before we exchanged our essence and the mate's promise."

See? This is why I love hanging out with Kennedy. Besides the fact that she's the only other human woman who lives in Nuit—though there's another pregnant one who visits occasionally to meet with the healer—she also knows what it's like to have been whisked away to this unfamiliar world. She read the spell, never expecting she would summon a demon, and when he showed up, he grabbed her just like Glaine did to me.

Like me, she didn't want to stay. Yet, here she is, and I have to ask, "What made you change your mind?"

Kennedy smiles. "Love did. I fell in love with Loki. And after that... he promised me loyalty. His love in return. These demons... they don't cheat. They're not hardwired that way. When they love, they love with everything they have. And they're immortal. That means, despite all evidence to the contrary, they're patient. They'll wait for you."

Funnily enough, I agree with her. Glaine... if I told him to wait for me forever, he would. Just so long as I don't insist I'm not his mate, he's not rushing me to do anything. I'm the one who can't stop thinking about taking things one step further.

I should've known I was a goner from that first bout of mate sickness the other day. If I'm being honest with myself, the more time I spent with Glaine, the more curious I became about the big demon. Whether it was because his absolute devotion to me directly caught my attention or the idea that 'fated mates' *might* be real... I don't know, but I'm drawn to him in a way I can't explain—and that I'm not so sure I want to fight anymore.

Now, kidnapping is not sexy. It's *not*. But when I remember that he's not human, that he doesn't have the same morals as we do, and that he's spent literal *centuries* searching for his fated mate only to believe that he found her in me... in his shoes, I might've done the same thing.

I'm attracted to him. Who would've thought that a hulking red-skinned demon with hair almost as long as mine would do it for me, but once I got past his alien features and just saw *Glaine*, I couldn't deny the pull I felt for him. The mate sickness just gave me the excuse to act on that attraction without feeling guilty for falling for him after he stole me from my kitchen.

I thought it would be a one-time thing. We took the edge off until we could get to Nuit and lose the chains. We did that. I'd hoped that meant the local mage would open up a portal and ship my butt back home, but that... that hasn't happened yet.

It's looking like it might never happen.

And here I am. Here's Glaine, who hasn't given up his vow to convince me that—should I choose him—he'll spend the rest of his life proving that I made the right choice. And while it's way too early to give in and agree to that, what about sex?

When I can't stop thinking about touching him, tasting him, *fucking* him... I can blame the mate sickness all I want, but the way I burn up when I think about seducing my virgin demon and letting him do a little more than pleasuring me with his mouth... I'm just as horny, only I'm in control of that. It's not like I'm gonna die if I don't bang him, but I really, really want to give it a try.

Is that because I *am* his mate? Maybe. Until I met Kennedy and Loki, I don't think I really grasped that a mating like ours could be possible. Oh, he told me that night in the dungeon that I'm not the first human to be fated for a Sombra demon. He's convinced that Sierra must be a mate to a hunter he knows, though he stole me away before he could confirm that himself.

He wants to be my mate. And though I can't promise him forever, not yet, maybe I can be his that way.

It's worth a shot.

CHAPTER 17
ANYTHING

BILLIE

Once I set my mind to something, there's no reason to wait to go through with it. That's why, later that night after Glaine brings home a dinner that one of the mated demonesses in the village made for us, I wait until we're winding down, ready for bed, before I look Glaine in his glowing green eyes and ask, "Would you like to take a bath with me?"

Since giving me his essence, I've learned that Glaine is a pro at locking down his emotions. It's as though he's steeling himself against the time I have to leave him. Now that I know about his history with Lilith, I understand him a lot better. I didn't need to peek at his past, either. Glaine still had his privacy, and after hearing the story from Lilith herself, it explains a *lot*.

All Glaine's ever wanted is his mate. He thought he found her once, only to watch her choose the most powerful male in his village. It didn't matter that he was a respectable soldier who had a close relationship with Duke Haures. In Nuit, Apollyon was in charge—and Lilith was *his* fated mate. Glaine couldn't stand in their way of their bonding—and the male I've come to know wouldn't if he could—but she left scars on his heart.

He's sure I'm his mate. For real this time. I doubt he'd understand the concept of rebound dating, and even if he did, it's been centuries since Apollyon and Lilith bonded. Considering the damage Trevor did to me, my undeniable attraction to Glaine is probably *my* rebound... but the more I think about doing this, the more I'm sure it doesn't matter.

I'm not trying to tie myself to Glaine forever. I mean, I've known him for a week. Declaring my love for a guy I barely met is Tandy behavior, not Billie. It took me seven months before I told Trevor that I did, and a month longer before I introduced him to Sierra. I need to take my time, and no 'fated' bond or mate sickness pushing me toward Glaine is going to change that.

But sex? Sex is different. It can be emotionally charged, but it doesn't have to be. It can be purely physical, too. I've had my share of one-night stands, just to scratch an itch. I encouraged Sierra to do the same before she was too famous for it to be feasible. I've never been shy, either. I'll proposition a guy if I'm down to fuck, and if he is, too... well, let's go.

But Glaine isn't just a random human guy, is he? Does he realize that, when I say 'bath', I'm not asking because I've changed my mind and want him to scrub my back?

Glaine closed himself off as soon as I invited him to join me. Me? I did my best to keep my thoughts and intentions open so that, if he dipped into my essence, he'd know that I was hoping the bath—with both of us naked and in close proximity—would lead to something more. I *want* it to. I couldn't offer him anything more than pleasure, but if he could accept that...

Our eyes meet. I see that same hunger that was there the night we met and he stole me away. I see straight-up lust. I see *need*... and, through the whisper of a bond stretching between us, I sense an excitement tempered with a touch of resignation.

Glaine knows. He knows that, if we have sex, it doesn't change anything; at least, not when it comes to my desire to get back to Sierra, or my insistence that I can't be his bonded mate. For now, though, we're stuck together in Nuit, chains or no chains. We're obviously attracted to one another in spite of our huge differences, and even if I can't give him forever, I can give him tonight.

And he wants that connection with me enough to accept that.

He simply bows his head, then turns to set the tub up. Just like the one the doppelseers' have, it fills up on its own, and empties the same. By the time I've stripped off my dress and pulled my curls up into a knot on the top of my crown, the slightly steamy water is at the right height for the both of us.

He starts to pour in the soap, but I stop him. I don't trust the local healer enough to risk a UTI, and since I don't know how far we'll go in the tub, we don't need the soap. After all, I'm not trying to get clean. I'm just trying to let my demon get used to my naked body.

Glaine is not shy one bit. As he climbs in first, sporting one hell of an erection, he puffs out his chest when he notices me staring at it. He's preening again, showing off his cock to me, and I let him.

More than that, I know that I made the right choice.

I join him in the tub, sitting on the opposite side. His legs stretch out past me, cocooning my much smaller form. I smile and tilt my head back, resting it on the edge of the tub as I close my eyes in bliss. Somehow, the water temp is always perfect. Refreshing when the heat of Sombra gets to me, but cooling me down when I'm hot and horny.

Glaine growls softly under his breath.

I smile.

Whoops. Does that have my tits up and out of the water? Maybe. When I peek over at him, is Glaine staring at them like a starving man?

You know it.

My smile widens as I move my foot. The best part about our height difference? When we're sitting in the tub, Glaine's legs on the outside of mine, my foot is nestled right in the crook of his groin. With the slightest flex of my ankle, I'm stroking the length of his dick.

He sucks in a breath at the first touch.

I look at him. "Is that okay?"

"My heart is yours, my Billie," he grates out, speaking through closed fangs as if it's all he can manage. "My body is, too. Learn your male. Touch him. You can do anything you want to me."

I'd hoped that would be his answer.

My smile turns wicked. "What if I want to use you instead of my false cock?"

He gulps. "Are you saying you will mate me?"

"Not bond," I say, hating that I have to clarify that, but knowing that I'll regret it—and so will he—if I don't, if he gets the wrong idea, and our first time together ends in his disappointment. "But if you're down... I'd like to mate."

Saying I'd like to fuck just seems wrong. It implies I only want him for sex, not because I care about him, and though I teased him about acting like my vibe... if only for tonight, I can be his mate.

His claws scratch against the tub.

I raise my eyebrows at him. "Is that a no?"

"If you are in need of your male because the mate sickness is being too powerful, I would rather use my mouth to give you pleasure."

Is that the problem? "Glaine. It's not because of the mate sickness. I feel fine." I move my foot again, using my toes to trace the thick vein in his shaft. "I just thought... maybe you want to do this. But if not—"

I try not to feel rejected. After all, I've been putting him through that since we met. Can I really be peeved that he's willing to go down on me instead? That was amazing, yeah, but because it was, I figured sex would be, too. I won't rush him, though. If he's not ready, he's not ready. Just because I thought I was—

I dropped my gaze to the water. That was my mistake. I looked away and Glaine... he surged from the water, gripped me by the waist with his shadow claws, and moved me. I squeal, expecting he's making good on his offer to eat me out, but instead of lifting me up to his shoulders, he plops me right on top of his cock.

It's trapped between us. The way I'm straddling him has my open pussy pressed against his heated flesh, but it'll take a lot more wiggling and maneuvering to take that thing inside of me.

I dig my nails into his chest, clinging to him.

He grins down at me.

"My mate requires her male, not because she is sick for him, but because she's chosen him on her own. Even if this is as close to mating as we get this eve, I have never been so satisfied."

"Hold on, demon," I laugh, the relief making me feel as light as Glaine thinks I am. "Don't go nutting already. I haven't even shown you the good part yet."

"As I told you, my body is yours. Take your pleasure. That's all I need to find mine."

We'll see about that.

Reaching between us, I grab his dick in my hand. He jolts, and I hear another scratch of his claws against the tub. I grin. So that wasn't a bad sign before. It was just a clue that Glaine was already close to losing his control.

Good. That means it won't take much for me to make that happen.

I rise up on my knees. Angling his dick, I wait until I feel the warmth against my entrance. The sensation is so unlike anything I've ever known that I pause for a moment just to let it sink in.

Then, before he can try to tell me that I don't have to do this if I don't want to—this close and this open, I couldn't resist tapping into his essence if I tried—I do the same.

I sink *down*.

It takes a couple of minutes. I coo soft assuring sounds so that Glaine knows that this is normal, that I'm taking my time fitting him inside of me, and once I'm halfway down, he relaxes his big body.

Oh, baby. He relaxed too early. Even though I haven't fully seated myself on him, I lift a little, squeeze, and drop further down.

Scratch.

I laugh. "Doing okay?"

His voice is impossibly deep as he says, "Never better, my mortal."

I let that one pass because he's staring at me with such awe on his face, no way is he trying to be dismissive. Instead, I tease, "I like the tub. After tonight, it's gonna be my favorite. I'd hate to see you claw it to shreds."

"I'm sorry, Billie—"

I'm not. "Here." I take his hand in mine and place it on my tit. "Try holding on to this. See if you can control your claws."

"For you, *anything*."

He said that so kindly, I offer him the second one. Then, once he's grabbing onto me, I start to move.

And I don't know if the demon gods of Sombra are anything like the one I grew up learning about in Sunday School, but I swear, Glaine sees *heaven*.

He really meant it when he said that I could use his body any way that I wanted to. The most he does—at my urging—is hold my breasts in his palms as I get used to him.

I'll admit: he's bigger than I thought, but still not as bad as Biff. I know he doesn't want to think about Trevor, but the fact is that I was having regular sex up until I met Glaine. It's not like it's been years and I need to be stretched out. I actually prefer this position because it lets me get used to him at my own speed.

Once I am, I turn all of my attention toward making him feel good.

And me, too.

Just as I'm about to explode on top of him, Glaine releases my tits before firmly gripping my ass cheeks. Pulling me to him, he rises up from the tub without even needing his hands to do it. Good thing, too. They're too busy kneading my flesh, holding me close, keeping me pinned on his length.

Water rushes onto the bedroom floor as he climbs out, taking both of us with him. Knowing how much he loves it when I play with his horns, I grab the first set on each side I can find and hold on tight.

We're both soaked. Glaine could easily use his shadow magic to dry himself off, and I have a spare piece of woven fabric that I've claimed as my towel. But instead of that, he lays me out on our bed, my back sticking to the covering as he bows his slick body over mine, working his hips.

It hits me in a flash what happened. I was riding

him in the tub, but he couldn't really do anything except take it. He is a dominant demon soldier. Of course he'd have the instinct to thrust into his female. Virgin or not, I'm thinking some things are just natural, and a male shoving his cock in and out of a pussy to chase his nut is probably one of them.

I don't mind one bit. I arch my back, moving my hands to his shoulders—or, really, whatever part of him I can reach—and enjoy the sensation of him quickening those thrusts.

It's funny, though. He looks so... so determined. His face is screwed-up, he's holding one of my legs around his waist so I can't get too far from him, while the other is pinned down, opening me as wide as possible for him.

Without me clutching his horns, he can bend his head to nuzzle my bouncing tits with one of them. He's careful not to gore me with them, but the way he's methodically playing my body right now? I don't think I would've cared.

I moan, and Glaine whispers my name like it's a prayer. As if all he needed was another sign that I'm into him, he starts pistoning his hips a little faster.

I gasp. "Glaine, *god*. What are you doing?"

"I am... what's the word? Ah, yes... I am *fucking* you, Billie."

I squirm. Glaine is always so solemn and commanding with his speech, only with a rare hint of humor. Even when we were intimate together the first time, he was more in awe than anything. Since meeting him, I've enjoyed the small glimpses of his playful side, but to hear him say 'fucking' like that when I rarely do?

Damn it, I *squirm*.

Because fucking me... that is *exactly* what Glaine is doing right now. His big body is covering mine, thick fingers wrapped around my ankle as he pins it against his pistoning hip. My other leg dangles off the edge of the bed he laid me out on. Too much in a rush to get back inside of me, Glaine tipped me onto the side of the bed instead of in the center. Or maybe this way he could open me up as wide as possible, fitting his hulking demon body in the cradle of my legs so that I can't do anything but take him.

I was so close in the tub. As Glaine starts to shake, my virgin lasting longer than I expected for his first time, I drop my hand to my clit. I want to go over the edge with him, and right now? This is what I need.

Glaine is a quick study. Noticing what I'm doing, he lets go of my ankle. Then, turning both his claws and most of his fingers to shadow, he replaces mine on my clit.

Holy shit. Holyshit. *Holyshit.*

It's like double the pleasure. His finger does the work while the edge of his shadows amplifies every sensation in my body. He's barely started before I'm keening, squirming closer so that I don't miss a single touch even after I'm spasming around his dick.

That's all it takes for Glaine. Roaring as he comes, he drops his head down to mine.

Well. What's that saying? In for a penny, in for a pound?

I clutch Glaine's jaw and I do something I've never done with a guy during sex unless it's when I'm in a relationship: I kiss him.

It doesn't matter that I surprise him. I figured he had no idea what I was doing, but since it was pleasurable, he went along with it. Until he checks my essence, he won't have any idea just what a big deal that was for me.

But I do. And with my fingers now tangled in Glaine's long, damp hair, our bodies so intertwined that I can't tell what part is mine and what part is his, I kiss him at the same time as I admit that Fate's more than got her hooks in me.

It's got a pair of claws and a demon dick in me, too.

And I'm not complaining one bit.

CHAPTER 18
REMORSE

GLAINE

ONE CYCLE LATER

We are on the cusp of the next gold moon, and I have yet to fulfill my mate bond with Billie.

In every other way, we are mates. We share the same bed. She welcomes me into her body. We eat together, laugh together, and exist as every other mated pair in Nuit. The only difference is that she is yet to give me her mate's promise, and until she does, I can't help but dread the moment she decides that she no longer wants to be mine.

She has all of Sombra to find a new male. Worse,

she can find a mage that does not respect Duke Haures enough to obey his laws. A rogue demon could bring Billie to the human world only to have Candor or Loki dragging her back in chains again.

I've kept her from the duke's dungeon. I've done the same for myself. She treats me like her mate. I should be content with all that, especially since this is my own doing. I thought of nothing but myself when I carried Billie through the portal and into my realm. I wanted her and I took her, and now she must stay here.

Unless I release her. Unless I stand by as Candor uses magic to erase the memory of me and her time in Sombra from Billie, allowing her to return to Earth with no knowledge of my world. She wouldn't be breaking the first law if she did, and the only one who would pay the price for my selfishness would be me. I'd only be fair, too, and the longer she refuses to give me the mate's promise, the more I feel... that I am remorseful. I am full of guilt.

I harmed the one soul that I should put above mine, and as the eves pass and, at the very least, Billie seems content with me, I regret that I was too impulsive. Too reckless. The grimoire was in Billie's quarters. The magic could have already been at work, pulling me toward her. Dagon was summoned by his mate. What could it have been? One moon? Two, perhaps, until Billie's kin left the book where Billie could find it and stumble upon the *verus amor* spell?

But I didn't wait—and now it seems as if that is all I've been doing.

She laughs when I mention that, in her world, we would've had to fulfill our bond by the first full moon. That when I went to warn Malphas of its approach, his human mate had one choice: be released or accept him as her male. They only had a few moons to decide, and Billie laughs, telling me that instalove doesn't exist, and you can't expect to know that you'll spend the rest of your immortal life with someone after a week.

I don't tell her that I knew she was the one for me in seconds. My essence does it for me, and if Billie clings to her odd belief that we should get to know one another without relying on mystical demon magic, I allow it.

I will do anything for my mortal.

Well, almost anything...

There is time. Even if she is not immortal herself yet, there is time, and forcing me to be patient is my penalty for what I did. So many of the lower ranks of demons—craftsmen and hunters instead of soldiers and mages—believe that there is a firm deadline when it comes to claiming a mate. That if you find your fated mate but don't bond to them by the next gold moon, then Fate got it wrong and you're both released from the bond, never to find another forever mate.

It doesn't work quite like that. Oh, there is some truth to their superstitions, and most of it stems from whispers of the human world of legend. Due to the first law that Duke Haures established two thousand years ago, if a mortal is destined to be a demon's mate, there must be an unbreakable tie between the pair before the duke interferes and severs it himself. That's where the urgency comes from; the threat of a life without their mate *and* a stay in his dungeons makes it so that a demon won't hesitate to prove themselves to their female.

In Sombra, demons still do so and, usually, the demonesses either accept their males long before the first cycle has passed—or they come to an agreement to release each other on their own without sacrificing the chance to bond to another. That's why the essence exchange usually occurs at the same time as the initial mating and the mate's promise. Once a male gives all he has to his female—and accepts her gift to him in return—there is no other chance. Even if they chose to petition the bondmaster to sever their bond, not even Duke Haures can give them a new one.

I want Billie. I will wait for her, and I will love her, and I will do everything I can to convince her that she should choose me to be her one true mate.

There is time—until, suddenly there is not.

WHEN THE KNOCK SOUNDS AT MY DOOR AND I SEE Apollyon wearing a solemn face, my heart lurches in my chest.

Billie is very popular among the other mated females in the village. When I'm patrolling the borders of Nuit with the clan leader, making sure our hunters return safely with their prey, and that none of the mindless prey beasts—such as the arkoda—attack from the edge of the shadows, she spends her time with Kennedy, Lilith, or Simra, one of the hunter's mates. All are currently without spawn, though Loki's mate is carrying his, and they drink javitz spiked with elderflower and chat when Lilith finishes lessons with the children for the day.

Apollyon did not need my company today. I was looking forward to seeing my mate, and telling her more stories of my time as a guard. Though she can simply look into my essence and see, my mortal loves to be entertained. We don't have a rectangle with moving pictures—a 'television', as she calls it—in Sombra, and while she borrows books from Kennedy and Lilith to keep from getting bored, her favorite entertainment is leaning back and listening to me rumble about my realm.

For a female who is so certain she cannot stay, she loves to hear about it. More than that, she admits she's enjoying herself. If only she didn't have responsibilities of her own in her world that she is determined to return to, our mating might be a smoother one... but she is happy for now, and that is all that matters to me.

I had prepared a story about a campaign in Brille Rouge, but before we could settle down with the lunch I made—since, for all Billie's blessings, cooking is not one of them—Apollyon knocked, and I knew from his face that he did not bring good news.

At least, not for me.

"Glaine. I hope I'm not disturbing you."

He is, but I'm careful not to tell Apollyon that. Not after all he's done for my mate and me. "Is there something you need?"

He clears his throat. "One of Duke Haures's mages is here."

I'd known this day would come. The doppelseers' magic concealed Billie and me while we traveled to Nuit, but it was Apollyon who—at Lilith's urging— offered us his protection. The duke accepted it, but the longer I live with Billie without fulfilling our mate... I'm not patient. Duke Haures? He's even less so.

I straighten my back. I'm also trying to block the door as Billie tiptoes behind me, obviously curious to the identity of our visitor. "For me?"

"No."

My heart skips a beat. "For Billie?"

He can try to take my mate, but I fear it won't be easy—

"Not quite."

I blink. "I do not understand."

Apollyon exhales roughly. "It is her kin. She is here."

Her... kin.

Sierra. The one soul I know that has my mate's affection and love. Her family.

And she's in Sombra.

In *Nuit.*

For a split second, I have the urge to slam the door in Apollyon's face. Maybe Billie didn't hear him. Maybe she doesn't know that her kin is near. Maybe I could hide her and keep her and—

No.

I am a better male now, and I am for my Billie. So, hiding any trace of panic rushing through me, throwing up a shield in case she tries to read my racing emotions, I glance over my shoulder to find her staring at me. Her lips are slightly parted, a very fetching shade of red coloring her pale cheeks. Her dim eyes seem glassy. Watery.

Are they leaking?

"Billie?" My voice is raw, and I gentle it as best I can. "Your kin is here."

That's all I need to say. As though a spell has been broken, her grin widens and, like I am not there at all, she pushes past me and runs out through the open door.

I try not to let it hurt as much as it does that she runs and never looks back at me once.

But I am a Sombra demon. I am pure shadow. Of course I shall follow her.

There are three figures standing beyond Apollyon: a human female with hair twisted the same way Lilith wears hers, and two demons. I recognize them both. The red-eyed hunter is Dagon, while the purple-eyed male with chin-length hair and stunted horns is another of Duke Haures's mages, Erebus.

I see three figures. My mate has eyes for only one.

"Sierra!"

"Billie!"

Just like I've suspected all along, Billie's kin must be Dagon's mate. The big hunter's eyes glow a fiery red as he hunches his shoulders. His possessive instincts are on display as he bares his fangs, but he stays where he is while the two human females collide while laughing, then embrace. He controls himself before his mate releases mine, but I know what I saw and am even more on edge than before.

At first, I think it's because he recognizes that Billie is a female like his mate and, therefore, no threat to his mating.

Then I see that he has something he's holding carefully with his claws. Is that... an ungez in a glass case? No... no. That is a 'cat'.

Ah. That must be Three.

I don't know what they are doing here. That Erebus is standing beside them as a portal winks out, it's clear that the mage brought them to Nuit. Brought them to my mate.

When a Sombra demon is summoned by the *verus amor* spell, a pathway exists between our realm and the human world for that demon. It's why I still cannot create a portal myself, despite knowing that Billie is my mate. But Dagon... he should've been able to bring his human mate to Sombra whenever he chose to after their bonding.

Is that what happened?

I get my answer in the next moment when Dagon's mate pulls back from Billie and says in a raspy voice full of emotion, "We've been looking for you everywhere! I went to the duke, he couldn't help at first, but then he said you might be here and he gave us a mage to zip us over and... holy fucking shit, B, you're here! I can't wait to talk to you. To tell you everything that happened! And, oh, you better spill the beans about what you've been up to, I swear to God."

"Sierra, Sierra, I can't believe it's you." Billie's head shoots over to Dagon. "And, damn it, he was right. Do you know how much I hate it when he's right? He gets so damn cocky and smug with that smirk of his... but he told me and I... look at you. You have your own demon mate, after all. Just like he guessed."

"I do. Dagon," beams Sierra. "What about you?"

I think that, at last, my mate cannot deny me. I know that I am the 'he' she mentioned, but instead of introducing me to her kin, she shakes her head. "We've got to talk."

"Okay. Where?"

Billie looks back at me at last. No. Not at me. She glances at the house, nibbles on her bottom lip with her blunt teeth, then shakes her head.

I don't know how to feel that she's rejected our home. That she's rejected *me*.

So I say nothing as Billie tells her Sierra, "Come with me. I know a spot by the fire pit that's gorgeous and we can talk."

I know of it as well. There are some nights when Billie makes a nest in the ash, watching the flames in the fire pit as if entranced by them. I go with her to make sure my mortal doesn't actually get burned, and she laughs as she tells me that watching the flames is the closest thing to that 'television' she misses.

I go with her because she is Billie, and I will follow her anywhere. But my mate also knows that I—like most Sombra demons—don't share her fascination with the fire. I tell myself not to be hurt that she does not invite me, and that there is no reason to worry since Dagon is joining the two females.

I tell myself that—and know that I am a liar.

I take a step.

Erebus lays his palm on my shoulder, a silent

warning to stay behind while another demon and his mate leave with my Billie, and though she is still in my sight for the moment, I know then that I have truly lost my mate... again.

But unlike what happened with Lilith all those years ago, I'm not sure I have the strength left in me to release Billie from our growing bond.

I love her. From the moment I caught her scent in her quarters, I knew she was born to be mine. The centuries I waited... every second brought me closer to the moment when the gods would reward me with my forever mate, and though I did not deserve one such as my wee mortal, I was prepared to do whatever it took to prove myself to her.

I tried. I attempted to be an honorable male, even when a Sombra demon's idea of what made him honorable differed from that of a human. But while I made missteps along the way, everything I did, I did because I loved her.

I love her smile because, when she favors me with it, I know that I've done something to earn it—even if it's in jest. I love how fierce she is despite being so tiny, and how I vowed to protect her only to watch in amazement as she protected *me*. I love how soft her cunt is, how easily she opens up to me as though part of her recognizes me as her mate while that most stubborn heart of hers holds out on me.

I love the way she curls up next to me while she

slumbers, showing her trust in her actions though she won't say it with words. The same with how she cares for me. I don't need Billie to say it. I have her essence, and if I did not, I *know* my mortal.

She cares for me... just not enough to stay.

I wish I had more time. Because while the gold moon might not have marked the end of my wooing Billie, now that her kin has arrived with her mate to whisk my Billie away, I admit that I do love her enough to let her go.

And as soon as she is gone and I no longer see her, I turn to Erebus.

"I assume the duke is expecting me?" I ask, holding out my hands as I do.

Erebus gives me a single jerking nod, visibly relieved that I will not fight my newest fate. He is a mage, a fact I know all too well when he begins weaving the enchanted chain at the same time as he builds a shadow portal behind him, and I am a guard.

I *was* a guard.

And now? I will be Duke Haures's prisoner once more.

BILLIE

I'm shocked. There's no other way to describe it. My head is whirring, I'm listening to Sierra tell me all about how she met her demon mate, and I know I'm making all the appropriate responses—"A grimoire in your fan mail? Who sent you that?" and "See? That's why I can't leave you alone. Summoning demons while I'm away from the weekend... that's so Sierra."—but I'm trying to figure out what this means, why she is here, and how this changes things for me and Glaine.

Because I have to be real here. Sometime after coming to Nuit and moving into his house, I started to accept that I might never go home. And I wondered: would it be so bad if I had to stay? Maybe if I was still in the dungeon, but I have a male who worships the ground I walk on *in shoes* because I finally have *shoes*, who loves me, and who—damn it—is the perfect guy for me.

He likes that I'm a ballbuster. That I need to have some kind of control. It took a while for him to realize that we get along better when he does, and as a soldier who is trained to be commanded, the two of us enjoy the other's company when we're not butting heads.

The sex is amazing. I'm not just saying that to boost his ego because he was an inexperienced virgin with seven centuries of pent-up need. To him, a good session is when he gets me off repeatedly, and if he has the chance to nut, he gets this expression on his face like he wants to *thank* me.

Glaine is *fascinating*. I think I like that more than his dick, though I'm definitely not complaining there. Not only does he have seven hundred years of life experiences, but he's the rare Sombra demon who got to leave his plane and visit countless others.

I thought I had him beat, having spent most of my life traveling all over the world. That's just *one*. Glaine's seen so many, and he tells me all about them. He doesn't make me feel stupid, either, or that he's humoring me when I get excited and ask him questions. Though I know he'd rather me rely on his essence—and I have been lately because, well, why not —Glaine enjoys teaching me about all the worlds he's been to, with the unsaid promise that, one day, maybe he can bring me.

Who knows what forever will bring, right? We're on Duke Haures's shit list now, but if I bond myself to Glaine and become immortal... who knows if he'll change his mind?

Because, honestly? I've been thinking about changing mine.

It was a slow process. And I'm sure people would think I was nuts if I said that me spending, like, a month debating whether I wanted to give Glaine forever or not was a slow process. But in a realm where demons and demonesses usually are bonded the same night they recognize that they're one true mates, keeping Glaine on my hook this long without giving him the mate's promise *is* unusual.

I just... it's not that I don't want to. I do. The more I've involved myself in village life, the more I've said my goodbyes to my old one in New York. I mourned Sierra. I've regretted that, after being my father figure for so long, Roy won't have any idea what happened to me. And Three... I miss my fluffy boy. But I could deal. I have Glaine. I've forgiven him for stealing me, and I'm actually kind of glad he did.

For the first time in years, I'm living my life for me. Not to get out of poverty, not because I signed a contract, and not because I was responsible for Sierra's. There are no calls on my time. I still get distracted sometimes and reach for my phone, as though I want to jot a note or snap a picture, but it's been a while since I've even thought of my former lord and ruler, the almighty schedule.

Which is why, after Sierra tells me the Cliff's Notes version of her story, and I go into autopilot to tell her mine—"I knew that guard demon had to take you! You never would've left your phone of your own free will!"—I gloss over much of it, feeling like I spend more time defending Glaine's actions than explaining to Sierra that, if she's happy with her mate, so am I.

But then she asks, "How long have you been here with him," and I realize that I... I don't know. Not really.

Ah, jeez. That's a good question. In New York, I lived my life by that calendar on my phone. Every single minute of every single day was planned down to the second, with every appointment marked down in my app. Ninety-nine percent of it had to do with my career as Whiskey Rose's manager where I couldn't risk screwing up because Sierra depended on me.

It honestly took days before I stopped automatically reaching for the phone I left behind when Glaine grabbed me. Even now, I still feel a little naked without it. I don't think I'll ever stop the habit of looking for my phone when I want to know something as simple as the time, and when Sierra asks me about how long I've been here, it rankles that I have no clue at all.

The village counts by cycles of the gold moon. We have another one coming up soon, but it seems a little longer than thirty days since the last one. I just... I guess I got so wrapped up with learning about life in Sombra—and living with Glaine—that I never bothered keeping track.

"A month, I guess. Give or take."

"Are you fucking with me?"

I shake my head. "I wish I was. I'm sorry," I say, the first time I apologize. But I need to. "You were probably so worried about me. I said I was coming home, I left my purse and my phone behind, but I was gone with no way to contact you. I had no idea that you had a demon in the apartment"—and I pointedly forget to mention that I thought the door was closed because of Jared—"or that you'd ever guess I was here in this demon world... but I have been ever since Glaine grabbed me."

"And I have a thing or two to say to him about that," Sierra says darkly. "But that's not what I meant. Me and Dagon, we were only back home for two days, finishing up..." Sierra's eyes dart to the left where her demon is still holding onto the clear bubble carrier that's holding a very sleepy Three. "Stuff. Had to get Three ready," she adds hurriedly before I can call her out on obviously hiding something from me, "and then Dagon took us to Caol to start our search for you."

"I wanted to show Sierra off to my clan," the demon says.

"And the tattoo that Duke Haures arranged for you to get before he let us leave the throne room," Sierra adds.

As if I could pretend my best friend isn't bonded to the red-eyed demon. The proof is in the pudding—or, in this case, the shimmering silver runes tattooed to the middle of his bare chest that spell out her name.

S-I-E-R-R-A.

"Anyway, when no one in Caol heard of a rogue guard and his human captive, er, mate," Sierra amends at my sudden look, "we visited two nearby villages. Nothing. Duke Haures told us that some kind of magic was keeping you hidden the first time I met him, but I went back for more intel. That was this morning. We left our suitcase and Three's food at the palace, then hitched a ride with that purple-eyed wiz to Nuit to see if the rumors were true and you were here. I swear, it couldn't have been more than a week for us."

Really? Huh. And I spent so long thinking that days were passing and people were freaking out over me once I started missing appointments, and while Sierra obviously came searching for me... it's been a week?

"I told you, my mate," rumbles Dagon, finally cutting into the conversation. "Time runs differently in Sombra depending on the duke's whims. The only constant is the gold moon."

"It's fine. It doesn't really matter now that we found you. We can go back, get our stuff, and be in the apartment in no time."

I stumble a few steps back, my curls falling forward in my face. "What?"

Sierra frowns. "I know that 'what'. B... you are coming home with us, aren't you? The duke said you weren't a mate. That you didn't get bonded to the demon who took you. He wanted you to have a little mindwipe, but his mate suggested you can come home with us and, because you're my bestie, you'll keep the secret of Dagon and Sombra for my sake." She reaches over, patting Dagon's middle. "My mate's got connections. He asked the duke's mate, she asked him, and everything's good now."

No. Everything's *not* good. "Sierra, I'm so glad to see you. I mean it. I love you. But... a lot can change in a month."

A sly look crosses her pretty face. "Let me guess. Could it be that you figured out that you *are* a mate?"

I shrug. "Maybe."

"Jeez, B. Really? And, what, you're gonna stay? Fuck it. Bring him back with us. The more the merrier."

"I wish I could. I don't know if the duke told you, but Glaine is not allowed to go to the human world anymore. And since he has to stay here, I think I'm going to, too."

And there it is. What I've been thinking of doing

these last couple of weeks... I've said it out loud. Now that I have? I have to admit that it was only a matter of time until I realized how much I'm looking forward to sticking around in this fascinating place while also having Glaine as *my* mate. Especially now that I know Sierra is bonded to Dagon and can come see me any time, I have the best of both worlds: the demon who got past my own prickly exterior, plus the best friend I could never lose.

Instead of trying to convince me to change my mind—because my lifelong friend knows that's impossible—Sierra wrinkles her nose. "You actually like that grumpy guard?"

"I love him," I say simply. Hey. Wait. "You know Glaine?"

She taps her temple. "You forget that I got Dagon's download. My demon worked in the capital city for, like, three decades. He had more than a couple of run-ins with Glaine in that time. So even if I've never met the guy, I feel like I know him... and I know that you don't get to pick your fated mate or anything, but you seem to actually like that sourpuss."

That's because I do.

"Honestly? He kinda reminds me of you, Sierra."

Dagon makes a sound like a choke.

Sierra raises her eyebrows at me.

"It's pretty easy to get along with him once you realize you can't let him steamroll over you. He may think he knows what's best, but sometimes I do, too. And"—here I grin—"he's learned that it can be pretty fun to let me take control."

Sierra matches my smile, a devious edge to it that is purely my best friend without a single hint of the pop star. "That's my Billie. All I've ever wanted was for you to find someone worthy of you." Her face hardens. "It wasn't Trev for you."

She doesn't know the half of it. I don't want to ruin our reunion by mentioning that fateful weekend and his confession to me, so I don't—though I do take her hand. "It wasn't Jared for you, either, Sierra."

Dagon growls under his breath.

"It's okay, demon," she murmurs even as she releases me. "Remember? She's my sister."

My heart swells because... well, I am, aren't I? And that won't change. In fact, with the two of us both having our own demon mates, I wouldn't be surprised if we get even closer.

"Forgive me, Sierra. But it is not your kin touching your hand that rouses my instincts. It is hearing the names of the males unworthy of either my mate or her kin." Another grumble, softer than the growl from before. "Trevor should've been left to the shadows. It's not too late for the pale-haired male to take his place."

"Huh. I guess he has your download if he knows about Trevor," I say. Hang on... "Assuming you mean

Jared when you say 'pale-haired male', I'm all for tossing him to the shadows. But why Trevor?"

I mean, *I* know why, but—

"Yeah. About that. I've been meaning to ask... when you told me that it might be a good idea to busy myself with my fan mail... you didn't, uh... I mean—"

"I didn't know there was a spell book in there, if that's what you're asking," I tease.

Sierra nibbles on her bottom lip before blurting out, "No, no. I was actually way more worried that you knew Trevor was writing me love letters that might've been in that bag."

Oh.

Oh, no.

I swallow roughly, losing my sudden humor. "I didn't." I say that as plainly as I can. I don't know how Sierra knows... "I only found out he wasn't who I thought he was on the night I disappeared with Glaine. That's why I was heading home from Connecticut. He told me... ah, shit, Sierra. He told me he was in love with you."

Her expression tells me that she already knew that, too. "Not me. Whiskey." She lets out a small laugh. "We had a lot of traffic at the Dorado that night. You. Glaine. *Trevor.*"

Wait. Trevor followed me from Connecticut to New York?

He was in our apartment?

"He—*what*?"

As I gape at her, Sierra tells me how Dagon sensed Glaine in the apartment. He was already gone—and so was I—when the demon went looking for him, and when Sierra then went tip-toeing after her mate, but they both found Trevor waiting on the settee in the living room. Dagon disappeared, Sierra confronted him, and my expression goes from surprise to horror to *furious* as she adds that, like Patrick Ridgefield, Trevor pulled a gun on her to convince her to leave with him.

"I'll kill him!"

"Dagon wanted to." She beams at her demon. "Almost did. Brained Trevor in with one of my Grammys. Luckily, that creep didn't see my demon, but he's locked up now, Billie. We don't have to worry about him."

If Sierra comes to stay with me and Glaine in Sombra, she won't have to worry about obsessed fans ever again...

Of course, I don't say that, though I wouldn't be surprised if she was thinking the same thing.

Sierra has thrown herself all in with her mate. I've done something similar with Glaine. We both know that she can't stay in the human world forever. She's immortal now. Eventually her public will notice she's stopped aging, and there's only so much she can blame on 'plastic surgery' in the future. Sooner or later she'll have to relocate here like Kennedy did with Loki, or, well, like I also did with Glaine.

But that's the future. I'm more than happy living in the now, and with my best friend here for the moment, I'm going to enjoy it—and that begins with bringing her to meet Glaine so that she can get a chance to form her own first impression on him without relying on Dagon's.

I should've invited him to join us when I dragged Sierra and Dagon over to the fire pits for privacy. Like I said, I was in shock. I wasn't thinking straight, and the only thing I *was* thinking was that the house I share with Glaine is *ours*. It didn't sit right with me to invite Sierra and her demon inside. Kinda like how we kept the apartment at the Dorado closed off because it was our personal space... that's how I think of the home I made with my mate.

I guess I expected he'd follow like always. That he didn't exasperates me at the same time as it charms me. He doesn't like going too far—a trait all Sombra demons share when it comes to their mates—but to give me time for my reunion with Sierra, he also gave me some distance.

Silly demon.

I gesture at Sierra. "Come on. I want to introduce you to Glaine. Three, too." We start heading back toward my home. "No matter how many times I try to explain the concept of cats and pets, he keeps thinking that Three is an ungez like Freya."

"Freya?" echoes Sierra.

"Kennedy's shadowy squirrel-cat." Seriously. That's the best way to describe Kennedy's pet. "Oh, right. You don't know Kennedy yet. You have to meet her. She's human, too."

And a huge Whiskey Rose fan, but that little reveal can wait. First, I need to find—

"Where's Glaine?" Weird. Our front door is open, Apollyon is still standing near the entryway, but there's no sign of my mate. That purple-eyed demon, either, though Lilith has joined Apollyon.

At my question, Apollyon glances at Lilith.

The motherly demoness turns her smile on me, and my heart sinks.

"Didn't he tell you?"

Um. No. "He didn't tell me anything."

"I'm sorry, Billie. But he returned to Mavro with Erebus."

CHAPTER 20
DÉJÀ VU

BILLIE

I didn't need Kennedy to bat her lashes and ask her mage mate to whip up a travel spell to take me to Glaine. I'm sure she would have if I'd given her the chance to, and I would've appreciated the help, but I'm Billie Bickles. I get shit done, and as I've learned over the last month, I don't need to have my phone to do it.

After I get Sierra's promise that she'll stick around until after I've gone after Glaine and—in a complete reversal of how we met—dragged his big butt back where he belongs, I go into problem-solver mode.

I trust my best friend. I'll miss not spending every day with her, but if Glaine is one hundred percent sure that he has to stay in Sombra, I can, too. For now, at least. I've only seen part of the palace and one village up close. Without the weight of being trapped here on my shoulders, I'd love to explore it some more—*with* my mate.

Because he's mine. I think part of me has always known that he was, from the moment he stepped out of the shadows and my first instinct *wasn't* to scream. I just hated the idea of fate taking the choice out of my hands. Being his fated mate, getting trapped with him in his demon world... I wanted to *choose*.

I could go back to New York. One day, I will. The upside of bonding with a demon is an immortal partner. With forever stretched ahead of us, there's not the same urgency to go home. With Sierra's confession that she's happy with her own demon mate, that she plans on retiring from show biz as soon as she fulfills her obligations, and the relief I felt at hearing that, while I fought to get back to New York to shield her from Trevor's obsession, she handled that without me... I can stay. There's nothing pulling me right back, and with Sierra having her own demon mate and a pathway back to Sombra, she can visit me as often as she wants.

She can bring Three, too, since our pampered kitty seems to lord over Sombra in the bubble backpack.

Who knows? I can have her adopt a cat for me and Glaine—maybe call it Four—or I can take a page out of Kennedy's book and tame one of the ungez like her pet, Freya.

There's so much I can do, and it starts with finding Glaine and letting him know that I'm ready to accept him as my mate. I'm sure, in his cocky way, he'll gloat that he was always right... but if that's the case, why did he so easily return to the palace without me when the demon duke summoned him?

I'm not sure, but I remember what he told Apollyon when we first came to stay at Nuit.

Where I go, she goes.

Same, demon. Same.

Right. Problem-solver mode. Glaine took a portal back to Mavro with a different purple-eyed demon. I grab Sierra, knowing how eager Kennedy will be to finally meet her idol, and basically throw my best friend at my new one. With both women distracted, and Dagon tending to Three in his carrier, I march over to Loki and jab my pointer finger in his chest.

"I have Glaine's essence. If you open a portal with your magic, can you bring me to him?"

Loki looks down his nose at my finger, already embedded in the first inch of his shadowy covering. He growls softly.

I don't give a shit. I dig my nail deeper, not bothering to hide my impatience. "Kennedy is spending time with another human mate. Trust me. She won't even know you've left if you hop to it, pal. Okay? Open the portal, drop me off, and if I have to walk back to Nuit with Glaine, just let Sierra know to expect me in a couple of days."

"Glaine is in Mavro—"

Duh. "I know that. I don't care. He needs to be here."

With me.

Loki's cheeks hollow as he stays silent for a moment. I know his story. Kennedy told me all about how he went demonic after a spell gone wrong, all because he was desperate to find his mate. He knows what it's like to be separated.

He also knows that, if a demon goes too far from his mate, he'll burn.

That happened to Loki. When Kennedy needed some space from him before they were bonded—but after their essence exchange—she tried to walk away, and he went up in smoke. That's how she discovered that the 'shadow' in shadow demon has two meanings: they can turn to shadow, and when they're trying to bond their mate to them, they *are* a shadow.

Is Glaine burning up now? When Kennedy would sit with me and Freya in her house while Glaine was helping Apollyon out as Nuit's security, she told me everything I could expect of being a mate. With a tablet from the village healer, he could extend the tether between us from ten feet to closer to a hundred-and-fifty... but Mavro is way farther than that.

Unless he's in chains again, dampening his demon aura, he might be, and that's all the more reason why I have to go to him.

Loki nods. "I will lead you through the portal. After that—"

"You can go. I'll be fine."

I'll be with my mate.

Up until the moment that Loki opens a portal on the other side and I get spat out from the shadows of his spell into very familiar surroundings, I think I convinced myself that Glaine took the first opportunity to be rid of me and high-tailed it back to the duke. After all, being the head guard *was* his identity. For centuries, that's all he was. Behind his shields, Glaine couldn't hide how much it hurt when Duke Haures released him from his duty. I should've known he'd go back if he could.

Isn't that what I was trying to do? Instead of taking the chance to have a new life, a new future, I was desperate to return to my old one. I was *the* Whiskey Rose's manager, right? I had the world at my fingertips. The power and prestige that came with the title... wasn't that what I fought so hard to see again?

That sounds terrible. Like I don't care about Sierra when the truth is that our lives were so intermingled, it was hard for us to just be Billie and Sierra. We were Whiskey Rose and manager. That's it. Having some time when I could *be* Billie again... it was good for me. Just like how I see the light in her eyes for the first time in years now.

She's happy with her mate. A workaholic to the bone, she won't dip on being Whiskey Rose and disappoint her fans, but she's looking forward to her future with Dagon.

And now that I've seen her and realized that I can have a life of my own, I want to share it with my own demon mate.

I only hope that I'm not too late. I wasn't playing hard to get all along, not really, and I regret to think I was leading Glaine on by acting the part of his mate these last few weeks without actually finalizing our bond, but I'm ready to do that now. So long as he'll still have me, I'll make him mine.

I thought my biggest obstacle would be that Glaine finally gave up on me and rejoined the other soldiers at the barracks—and then I see the narrow cat, the bars on the cell door, and Glaine crouched in the far corner, the front pair of horns in his chained hands, and I gasp.

I was wrong. *Way* wrong.

The portal closes behind me, but I don't care. If we're right back where we started, that's fine.

We're together and that's all that matters.

"Glaine?"

At the sound of his name in my voice, his head jerks up. "Billie. No. What are you... you're supposed to be in the human world. Not here."

Forget where I'm supposed to be... "What are *you* doing here? In the dungeon. In *chains*? I thought the duke dropped all the charges." Wait. A terrible idea pops into my head. *Supposed to be in the human world...* "Did you think I was leaving with Sierra? I just wanted to talk to her, Glaine. That's all. I wouldn't leave without you."

He blinks. "But I thought—"

"You thought wrong. And, baby, you shouldn't think without me there to help you out. What happened? You got the idea that I was leaving, and what? Since that breaks the first law, Duke Haures threw you back in the cell?"

"That's not why I'm here."

I raise my eyebrows. "Then why are you?"

"The duke's first law is that no human should know of Sombra."

"Unless they're a mate." I gesture at myself. "Mate."

Smart demon. He doesn't remind me that, technically, we're not fully bonded yet so it wouldn't count in the duke's eyes. It should, though. We got in trouble in the first place because I pointedly refused to accept that I was a Sombra demon's mate.

That was last month Billie. This month Billie? I'm proud to call Glaine mine.

"There are more laws than that," Glaine admits. "I was sent to put a clan artist in chains and take him to the dungeon once when it became clear that his human mate did not want to choose him. He kept the bond open and unfulfilled as long as Duke Haures allowed, but we demons have to accept when Fate and the gods get it wrong. Lilith denied me because she knew Apollyon was her male. And you... I'd wait forever for your acceptance, my mortal. But I won't put you through that now that you can leave me behind."

Is he... is he serious? The self-centered demon who stole me before he even said 'hi' is trying to be noble and let me go all because he got the wrong idea in his head?

"Oh, no, you don't."

The flash of obvious anger in my voice has Glaine's familiar scowl returning. "Excuse me?"

"You heard me, Glaine."

He pretends as though he didn't. "Why did you send... Loki. It had to have been Loki. Why did you send him away? You know I don't have the power for shadow travel. I am a... *was* a soldier. Not a mage. There won't be any guards willing to leave the cell open for me now. You should've left while you still could."

"And leave you in the dungeon?"

"Don't worry about me. We're not bonded," he says, and it's true. "No matter what's passed between us... I can release you from our mate bond. You no longer have to be tied to me."

"And that'll get you out of the dungeon again? You'll dump me to get free from the chains, that it?"

Was I wrong in believing that he honestly chose *me*? Not because of Fate, but because—

"No. Because I love you too much to keep you here when you don't want to be kept, my Billie. I love you enough to grant you the one thing you desire above all." He gulps, and I know he's remembering the prophecy from the doppelseers when he says: "Your freedom."

I never wanted freedom, unless he's talking about the freedom to choose. And guess what, Glaine?

"We're not bonded," I say, and he shudders out a breath to hear that I've agreed with him. I move closer to where he's still crouched. "At least, not yet."

His eyes brighten. "Billie?"

"You're not falling on your sword for me, Glaine."

A look of confusion flashes across his face as he slowly rises. "My sword? Would you like to take it for protection in the mortal realm? Without me there to keep you safe and your mortal body so fragile... I cannot retrieve it now because of the chains, but later—"

"Don't be an idiot. I'm not trying to stab you, I'm trying to keep you from sacrificing yourself for me."

Glaine juts out his chin. "I'm only upholding my end of the deal I made with Duke Haures."

What? "You made a deal with the devil? When?"

Glaine sucks in a breath, then exhales it roughly. Right. Probably not the best idea to refer to the ruler of his world as the devil, especially while we're under his palace, but come on. If Sombra is a Hell knock-off, that makes Haures the white-skinned version of Satan—especially if he sent another of his guards to take Glaine back to Mavro in chains.

My demon mate doesn't answer me other than that. That's fine. I've gotten to know Glaine well enough to know that, while he's proud, he's also protective. Considering the way I insulted the duke and it's possible one of the guards—or the duke himself with his strange magic—had overheard, he'll stay quiet if he thinks he's doing it for me.

Luckily for me, I have his essence.

I don't use it enough. It never sat right with me. Blame it on spending all those years in the tabloids, but even after I purposely stepped out of the limelight, it always irked me how people thought they knew me based on what they read online or printed in a magazine. People rarely got to know *me*, and that sore spot kept me from fully accepting the essence of who Glaine is because it seemed like... cheating, I guess.

The more time I've spent in Sombra, the more I've realized that I had let my own hang-ups twist something sacred to Glaine and his fellow demons. By giving me his essence, it was inviting me into his soul, giving me a front-row seat to everything *Glaine*. I'm not the one who stubbornly refused it for reasons that started to seem silly a few weeks ago.

So, though my first instinct isn't to tap into Glaine's essence and learn the answer for myself, there are times when I do and it's almost a natural reaction. If it saves me from being blindsided like when I learned he thought Lilith might be his fated mate, it's worth it.

I screw up my face. Through the whisper-thin bond that sprang up between us the first time I accepted that he might just be my mate, Glaine sends a jolt of pure love and undeniable panic toward me. His face gives nothing away, grumpy as ever, but his emotions are as clear as the memory of Glaine agreeing to return to the dungeons in my stead if I ever chose to leave and go to the human realm without him.

Because that's how Haures enforces the penalties for breaking the first law. Humans aren't allowed to know that Sombra or its inhabitants exist. The only exception, of course, is when a human female accepts that she is a Sombra demon's one true mate. Once the pair is bonded, they're both tasked with keeping Sombra a secret if they choose to exist together in the human world, like some of the mixed mated pairs have. But they have to be bonded—and while I haven't spent a night out of Glaine's bed since we left the bathtub together and tumbled into it, we're not bonded.

Well, that's about to change.

Even before he knew anything about me, he knew I was his mate. That's why he stayed behind in the throne room with Duke Haures while I was brought down to the dungeon that first night. Because he bartered with the duke—and Glaine's imprisonment is more because he thought I was leaving than because it's taken us this long to fulfill our bond.

I get the feeling that these rules of Duke Haures's... they're not laws. At the very least, they're not set in stone. As the ruler of Sombra, he can pick and choose who has to follow them, and what the outcome from not following them is.

Then again, if he's only here because he thought I was leaving, then once I prove to him I plan on *staying*, there's no reason for the duke to keep him down here.

That's a problem.

Solution: prove with actions more than words that I mean it when I say I'm not leaving.

Well. Here goes nothing.

CHAPTER 21

PROBLEM SOLVER

BILLIE

When it became obvious that I wouldn't be leaving the village for a while—if ever—Glaine went and spoke to the clan seamstress, Raiga. He offered to use coin to buy a few dresses that would fit me. Most of the demons and demonesses who live in Nuit don't use money, not like they do in the capital city. She didn't want his coin, and when he said he would find something to barter, she refused that, too. As a soldier, he left Nuit to keep Sombra safe—and, to the smaller clans that are often the first targets when demons rise up against Duke Haures, his lifelong service was more than enough to earn him three woven dresses to replace that red one I spent my first week in Sombra wearing.

I slip one side of the sleeveless dress I have on off of my shoulder. There goes the next. With a little hip wiggle, the dress shimmies down, pooling on the dungeon floor.

There isn't underwear in Sombra. The next time Sierra pops in, I'm getting all of my lingerie from the apartment, but for now... the dress is off and I'm completely naked.

Glaine rumbles under his breath. "You are uncovered, my mate."

I cup my breasts, rolling my nipples between my fingers. A teasing smile plays on my lips as I have his enraptured attention. "I'm *naked*, Glaine."

He shudders. "You are the most beautiful creature I've ever laid eyes on. But, I must confess, Billie... if any other demon spies you like this, I don't think I will be able to stop myself from reaching for my sword."

My smile widens. "And remind the duke that you have it? You're not a guard anymore. He might take the sword back."

"Let him." His voice is ragged as he watches me push my tits together, highlighting my cleavage. "I've given centuries of service to him. All I ever wanted was my mate. The sword... the prestige... my command. My freedom, even. I'd sacrifice it all for my mate." He swallows roughly, and I can't tell if it's emotional—or if the way I'm skimming my hands down my sides before settling them on my bare hips is arousing him beyond belief.

"Oh? And what would you do if she was right here in front of you?" Keeping one hand on my hip, the other dips between my legs. I finger a golden curl, showing him how damp it is. My pussy? It's soaked. Just watching him devour my naked body with his gaze has me turned on.

And, okay, maybe it's the chance that we could have a visitor any second now. Luckily, that's easily remedied...

Glaine voice drops. "I'd go to my knees and worship her the way she deserves to be worshiped. She's my gift from the gods, my one true mate, and deserves the worlds. Both of them."

I move toward him, closing the gap between us. "What if I told you that I only want to stick around one world for now?"

His expression shadows over. "So I was right. For the final time, you're denying me. Just like the prophecy foretold."

Glaine and that damn prophecy. Of course he doesn't think that the world I'm choosing is Sombra.

I'm standing directly in front of him. Instead of trying to explain, I decide to do one better.

I go up on my tiptoes, angling my head back so that I can invite his kiss. It's so funny when you think about how he had the instinct to put his mouth on my pussy long before I taught him just how pleasurable it could be to press my lips to his, slipping my tongue into his mouth so that I could stroke it.

Like I do now.

When I'm done, I keep my mouth right next to his.

"The prophecy was bullshit," I whisper against his lips. I have his essence. I know how much he believed in it, but it was a stupid riddle that, in the end, was worthless.

He gave me the freedom to go. I'm making the choice to stay.

"Billie?"

I cup his jaw. "Wrap me up in your shadows."

When he hesitates, I know it's not because he takes umbrage at anyone other than the duke giving him orders. I don't count. I can tell him to do anything, and if he can, he will. Using his essence, I can sense his confusion.

That's okay. I think I can explain.

"If you go from your solid form to your shadows, you can hide me with them, right? And if you do, no one can see me like this."

"But the chains—"

Hasn't he figured out the loophole yet? Probably not, since the duke has used Glaine as his muscle for centuries. If he's sent Glaine and a mage along to chain up demons for all that time, why would they second-guess him? But I've been thinking about that. The day that the rogue came at us, Glaine broke free of the chains by feeding it his essence. He didn't want to spare anymore—not if he wanted to give it to me—so he didn't do that again.

Now he doesn't have any because *I* do. I have his essence, and because I'm *not* a Sombra demon, I don't burn when I grab the chains and, with a soft *clink* and a tiny sting, they fall off, clattering as they hit the floor.

"How did you do that?" he marvels. "Are you a mage, my Billie?"

Hardly. "I just figured, you don't have demon essence to feed the chains. I do, thanks to you, but humans don't burn if they break the rules." If we did, it would've been Kennedy on fire with Loki. "I figured, I'll share a couple of drops to get you out of the chains. It stung, but I'm fine. And now we need to hurry before they come back."

"That is amazing." Glaine pauses for a moment. "But what if you had burned?" He reaches out with his free hands, clutching my elbows. "I would've lost you."

It's a good thing I didn't. And once I'm immortal, he won't have to worry about that anymore.

"But you didn't. Now, before those chains come back..."

"You are brave," he says, back to marveling again. "And you are wise."

"See? That's why you need human mates, babe. We bring a whole new perspective to Sombra."

"Like being unclothed in a demon cell?"

I pat him on the chest. "Or hiding in your shadows so that no one will know that I am."

He takes the hint. Without the chains, he dissolves into his shadows at my request even as he asks, "Wouldn't it have been easier to tug your dress back on?"

Maybe, but not if I want to do *this*.

I motion for him to drift a little lower. He does, I squint at him, then grab his shoulders, hoisting myself up knowing that, no matter what, he'll be there to catch me.

Even in his shadows, I can make out the outline that is my mate. After the last few weeks, I know where to find his cock—just like I know better than to think I won't find him hard and ready.

He sucks in a breath as I grab him there next, angling him until the head of his cock is tucked inside of my heat.

Then I meet the strained yet hopeful look on his shadowy face.

"If you don't want to do this, tell me. Not with your essence. With your words. I know you'll never deny me, and I want you to know that I'm not gonna do that to you, either. But if you don't want me to fuck you right now... to promise myself to you... then tell me. I'll find another way to get the chains off and get you out of here."

I mean it. I need to hear him say the words. I need to know that it's not his demon instincts that have him eager to bury himself inside of me, or the promise of sex that makes him want to take a mate.

Glaine palms my ass cheek with one hand. With the other, he lays his palm on the small of my back, pushing me gently at the same time as he jerks his hips, filling me halfway with his shadow dick before he nuzzles his chin on the top of my hair.

"I love you, my Billie," he repeats. "And I've made you the mate's promise in my heart every second of every day since the distrust in your eyes turned to affection. You say to use my words. Then I shall." I'm fully seated on his cock, stretched out deliciously as he dips his chin lower, rubbing it along my temple. "My soul will be yours." A kiss to my cheek as he withdraws about an inch of his cock before thrusting back up into me. "My heart is in your hands." He moves his hand from my back, slipping it between our bodies. He holds my breast, squeezing it just enough to have me gasp loudly... or maybe that's the sincerity in his words as he finishes his promise: "Our lives will be forever intertwined. I give myself to you. I give you everything."

On the word 'everything', Glaine pulls out halfway, then slams back in. I bounce on top of him, digging my nails into his chest.

"Yes," I whisper, arching my back as I press my groin against his, getting as close as possible. "*Yes.*"

He stills for a moment. "But that's my promise. You've had it all along. Without your words—"

Oh. Right. I was so distracted by how good that felt, I forgot this wasn't just sex for fun. We'll have plenty of that, but this is different. It's *important.*

So, clinging to Glaine, I tilt my head up and repeat everything he just said to me.

The second I do, something snaps into place. And though I've seen firsthand what a truly demonic demon looks like, I get a glimpse of it in *my demon* when he groans, then spins on his heel, searching for somewhere to lay me down.

The cot is narrow and small. It could never fit two figures side by side, even if one is a measly human. But with me on my back, and Glaine using one leg as purchase on the floor to pin me to the bed... we fit well enough.

"I knew it," he says, panting softly as he quickens his strokes, rocking into me as though knowing that our bond won't be completely finalized until he nuts inside of me. "All along, I knew you were meant to be my mate."

I grin up into the focused face of my demon. Everything, from those vivid green eyes to the double pair of horns that I will *never* allow him to hide again, belongs to me. No one else. And maybe that makes me selfish to think like that at this moment, but that just means that the two of us were truly meant to be because, well, isn't he doing the same?

We'll have to figure out how to get out of here. Now that we're bonded mates, Duke Haures has no reason to keep Glaine in the dungeon, and if it turns out fucking in the cells is frowned upon, I'd rather us be on our way before I find that out. The shadows are hiding everything that counts in case a guard *does* come to check on us, but at the rate that Glaine is racing toward his orgasm—and his shadowy claw rubbing my clit to help me on my way—he might be expecting them to pop their horns in soon.

For now, though? I enjoy this moment while it lasts. After all, it's only the beginning of forever—and after everything we've been through since I was grabbed by the guard, we definitely deserve it.

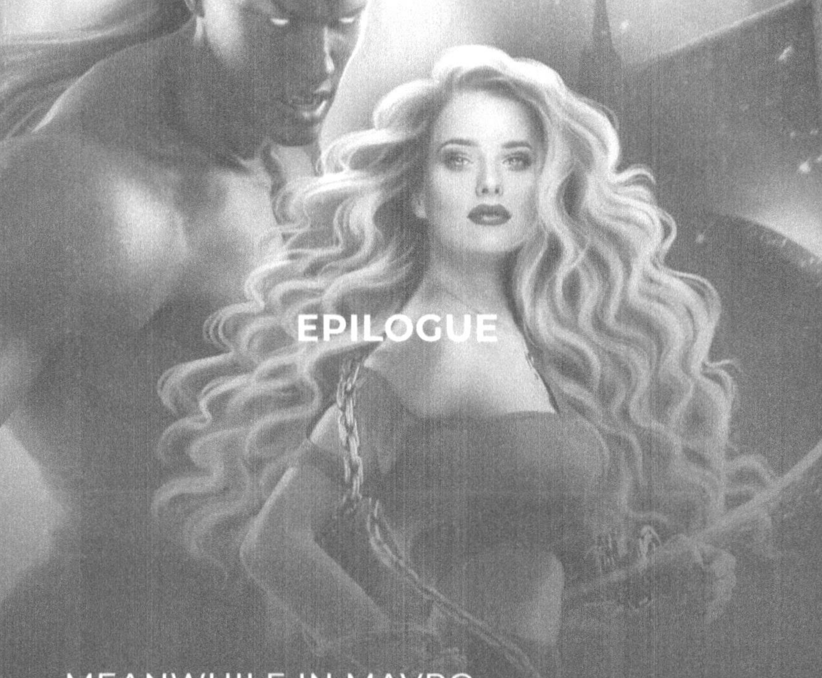

<h1 style="text-align:center">EPILOGUE</h1>

MEANWHILE IN MAVRO...

Haures tilts the crystal crown on his head, nestling it against the base of his horns, a small smile tugging on his lips as another bond snaps into place.

It took the first hundred years of his existence to learn how to control his power. To ward against the crowded village he was born into, the odd colorless demon left as a sacrifice to the shadows. Only the shadows were even more afraid of him than his fellow demons, and he stayed with his adopted kin until he knew that he would do better if he found solitude where the bonds didn't pluck at his white skin constantly.

For the first hundred years, he built the ward. For the next hundred years, he built a home in Mavro.

By the time he was three centuries old, he'd challenged the previous ruler—King Yelios—for his crown and his throne, taking both back to Mavro after Haures triumphed over Yelios...

That was two millennia ago. To this day, Haures wears the same crown, parks his rump on the same throne, and he lords over the demon realm for the same reason as he has done for the ages before: because it makes him the most powerful Sombra demon in the entire realm.

And he clings to that power because of *her*.

He waited two thousand years for *her*.

He made the arrangement he had with the doppelseers because of...

Haures glances down at his mate. She's curled up against him, her naked back nestled against his side, her tanned skin and black hair standing out against his starkly pale coloring.

As always her nose is in a book. Even after he had her keening from pleasure, panting his name, once he finished and tucked her against him, she stretched and yawned and reached for another book from her bedside table.

His mate hungers for knowledge. She thirsts to learn. Susanna loves him—the gods know he's so fortunate that she does—but after these years together, he knows that she'd give up the palace, the power, and their titles in an instant if given the choice so that he wouldn't feel the need to hide her in order to protect her... but she could never give up her access to the royal library.

Probably not the garden, either, Haures muses as he drops his hand to her ass, trailing a blunt claw over the nearest curve.

She arches back into him, chuckling under her breath even as she turns the next page.

Susanna's soft laugh has always been able to soothe something sharp and jagged inside of Haures. Even when he was unsure why the gods tempted him with her... when he tried to keep his distance because he knew, deep down, that he would never be worthy of her... her laugh reminds him why he stubbornly held onto the crown for so long, knowing that he might *not* be worthy of her—but that, as the duke of Sombra, his title and station would be enough to at least keep her safe.

And if it wasn't? Then his claws and tusks would be...

Haures knew from the moment Lucian and Damien approached him two thousand years ago that —like most demon males—he would do anything to find his mate, and to keep her. When the doppelseers admitted that the day would come that his mate would be from the legendary world of humans, as would theirs, a plan was forged. The first draft of the matefinder spell was written, and the *Grimoire du Sombra* was bound.

And then, for nearly twenty centuries, they waited. With the path between the human world and Sombra monitored, and the first law set into place, Haures ruled over Sombra, careful to conceal that his fate would, one day, be entwined with the mortal realm.

As would the doppelseers'...

It began with Susanna. His mate has a fondness for a human game called dominoes. That's how he can explain the doppelseers' connection to his beloved mate. A hundred human years after Haures brought the grimoire to Earth, waiting for his mate to be born and find it, she read the *verus amor* spell and set the events of the last three decades into motion.

There was Susanna, the first human mate to have crossed into Sombra since Haures became Duke Haures.

The first domino.

Amelia. Susanna's kin, and only a spawn when she summoned Nox to the human realm. Of course he had to imprison the hunter when it became clear that he needed to give the child time to mature. They still lived together in the human realm, though—if only for his mate's sake—Haures waited until the day they would return to Sombra to stay.

The second.

More time passed, and when Damien saw that the grimoire would pass hands rapidly, Haures sat on his throne and waited some more.

The clan artist from Nuit and his feisty pale-haired human.

The former rogue who, like Haures, escaped the shadows to claim his human mate and settle down with Apollyon's clan on the edge of Sombra.

Haures lost his former head mage when Sammael used the grimoire to summon his own mate, and now he and the bold human who retrieved the ashbalm flower are still in the human realm.

Then Susanna lost her own personal guard when Dagon chose to do the same. He might have returned to Sombra with his tawny-haired female in order to search for her missing kin, but Haures sensed the portal opening to Earth earlier this eve. Dagon and his mate are back in the human world.

His mate's kin and Glaine are not.

The latest domino has just fallen into pace, though, with the most recent bond snapping. And, with that, Haures's grin widens.

There is one final tile to go before the demon duke of Sombra can fulfill his side of the agreement that was set into motion two thousand years ago.

Damien saw this as well. When all Haures wanted was a mate and a child to carry on his legacy, he became the most powerful demon in the entire realm so that—because of his strange appearance and terrible magic—they would forever be protected. But while it was safe to claim Susanna as his when he finally accepted that the fragile human female *was* his mate, he could never allow himself to forget the second half of the doppelseers' prophecy.

But it would all change when that final domino fell. When Lucian and Damien—who saw the promise of their future the same day they saw Haures's—found their human mate in a female who would only summon them after seven other human females did first.

And then, when that vision has come to pass, Haures can finally breathe a sigh of relief and share his beloved Su with the rest of Sombra.

Well, no, he corrects as he shifts his bulk, throwing his leg over Susanna's, nestling his stirring cock in between her thighs... he will never share her, but he looks forward to the day when he'll no longer have to hide her from his people.

Susanna glances up from her book. Her expression warms over as she glances behind her. "Again?"

Haures grins, showing off his tusks. "Glaine has finalized his mate bond with his former mortal." Using a free claw, he trails it over the first rune in her name carved on his chest. "You know how... mm... randy your male gets when he senses mate bonds at work."

As if he needs an excuse to turn to his mate. But it's

true, and also a reason why he learned to block his fellow demon's bonds as early as he could. Between accidentally severing them or rubbing his cock raw before he learned control, it was torture for a demon already used to being kicked into the ash fields.

Until he became the strongest, most terrifying Sombra demon of all, that is.

Except, of course, to *her*...

Susanna's dim eyes—something that took Haures longer to get used to than he cares to admit—light up at what he said... and what he *didn't* say. They don't glow, but he sees the hope in them, and makes sure to return it ten-fold as his own eyes gleam.

"Not that much longer than, is it, my love? Until we can finally start a family of our own."

The next gold moon approaches. It might be too soon for Damien and Lucian to find their human mate, but with the dominoes falling faster and faster, there won't be that many left where he will have to abstain from enjoying his delectable little mate.

And since it's not quite the gold moon yet, and Susanna is always ready to welcome him so long as they're not risking the second half of the prophecy coming true... Haures angles his hips, lodging the head of his cock into her waiting heat.

He dips his head, nuzzling his chin against the top of her ink-colored hair as he slowly begins to feed his length into the one cunt meant to take it.

"Not much longer, no," he rumbles, a rare chuckle of his own escaping as Susanna clutches his thigh, moaning gently as he finds his way home again. "But, until the final mate finds her way to Sombra, I see no reason we should get out of practice. What do you say, mate?"

Susanna angles her head back, reaching up so that she can stroke the edge of his hard jaw with her delicate hand. "That I only hope the next girl doesn't make Damien and Lucian wait as long as poor Glaine had to..."

I always knew I was too much Tandy for one man... but what about two demons?

After another Christmas alone, I was preparing for a New Year's Eve party when I got the text that changed my life. Next thing I know, I'm bursting in on my old bandmate—and former friend—only to discover her apartment is empty.

Well, empty-ish. Because, as nosy as ever, I snooped a little... and that's when I found the old book that I've been dreaming about since I was a teen.

I don't really know why I'm so drawn to it, or how

the hell Sierra got her hands on it, but I can't help myself. I flip it open and start reading a random page, and that's when *they* appear.

Identical. Huge everywhere, and I'm not just talking about their horns, either. Made of shadows and with eyes glowing brighter than Times Square, they each grab one of my hands and away we go.

Where? Turns out they're from this immortal demon realm where they've spent more than two thousand years waiting for the one woman meant for them alone: *me*.

I've never had a partner who wanted me for me. I've been the other woman trashed in the press, and the one discarded for someone better. The idea that these big demons are utterly devoted to me is tempting —and so is how... *eager* they each are to convince me to choose him.

Throw in the offer of immortality and I'm thinking this might not be so bad... until I find out there's one teeny-tiny bit of fine print they forgot to mention.

Because demon twins are rare, and one thing that makes them different than any of the other monsters in this place?

Is that they have to *share* theirs.

And me? I'm the lucky chick who's supposed to belong both Damien *and* Lucian.

Taken by the Twins is the seventh book in the **Sombra Demons** series. It tells the story of Tandy, a party girl who's ready to settle down, and the twin demons, Damien and Lucian, who are more than happy to share their new mate.

KEEP IN TOUCH

Stay tuned for what's coming up next! Follow me at any of these places—or sign up for my newsletter—for news, promotions, upcoming releases, and more!

SarahSpadeBooks.com
Sarah's Newsletter
Sarah's Signed Book Store

facebook.com/sarahspadebooks
x.com/stressie
instagram.com/sarahspadebooks
amazon.com/author/sarahspade

ALSO BY SARAH SPADE

Holiday Hunk

Halloween Boo

This Christmas

Auld Lang Mine

I'm With Cupid

Getting Lucky

When Sparks Fly

Holiday Hunk: the Complete Series

Claws and Fangs

Leave Janelle

Never His Mate

Always Her Mate

Forever Mates

Hint of Her Blood

Taste of His Skin

Stay With Me

Never Say Never: Gem & Ryker

Bound by the Moon

Sombra Demons

Drawn to the Demon Duke*

Mated to the Monster

Stolen by the Shadows

Santa Claws

Bonded to the Beast

Fated to the Phantom

Claimed by the Creature

Grabbed by the Guard

Taken by the Twins

Shannon in Sombra

Stolen Mates

The Alpha's Heart*

The Feral's Captive

Chase and the Chains

The Beta's Bride

Wolves of Winter Creek

Prey

Pack

Predator

Protector

Sanctuary

Watch Me Burn

Make Me Bleed

Claws Clause

(written as Jessica Lynch)

Mates *free*

Hungry Like a Wolf

Of Mistletoe and Mating

No Way

Season of the Witch

Rogue

Sunglasses at Night

Ain't No Angel

True Angel

Ghost of Jealousy

Night Angel

Broken Wings

Of Santa and Slaying

Lost Angel

Born to Run

Uptown Girl

A Pack of Lies

Here Kitty, Kitty

Ordinance 7304: the Bond Laws (Claws Clause Collection #1)

Living on a Prayer (Claws Clause Collection #2)

Diamonds are a Witch's Best Friend (Claws Clause Collection #3)